Life does not change, people do;
learn to accept that not everybody is
who you thought you knew.

On The Inside

Vasundhra Atre

VISHWAKARMA
PUBLICATIONS VP®

On The Inside

First Edition - August 2016

© Author

ISBN - 978-93-85665-21-9

The views expressed in this book are those of the author and do not necessarily represent the views of Vishwakarma Publications.

This is a work of fiction. Names, characters, businesses, places, events and incidents are either the products of the author's imagination or used in a fictitious manner. Any resemblance to actual persons, living or dead, or actual events is purely coincidental.

Published by:
Vishwakarma Publications
283, Budhwar Peth, Near City Post,
Pune- 411 002.
Phone No: (020) 20261157 / 24448989
Email: info@vpindia.co.in
Website: www.vpindia.co.in

Cover, Typeset and Layout
Chaitali Nachnekar - Vishwakarma Publications

Dedication

To my doctor friends,

Never get so busy making a living that you
forget to live

Acknowledgement

The process of publishing a book is not the function of one individual. The idea for the book is a chance word, an expressed thought or a flash. Thereafter, it is the patience of the people around you that sustains you as you convert that single thought or word into pages; the critical appraisal from family and friends and then the confidence of a publishing house that ensures that the written word sees the bookstand.

The process is made all the more pleasurable by those who believe in and encourage you. I would like to thank all those who accompanied me on this journey.

My family as always who support me in all my endeavours. Special thanks, to my niece Aditi, for her analytical read and her christening of the book- 'On the Inside'.

My friends for believing in me. I would like to especially thank my very good friend Deepa Soman for her continuing support and critical edit.

Many thanks to Shivani, Gayatri and Chaitali for all their valuable inputs. I am grateful to my publisher Vishwakarma Publications for their faith in me and for ensuring that the book reached the bookstand in the promised time.

Word from the author

Medicine- a noble profession, is a thought that has been echoed and re-echoed. Those practicing the art and science of medicine find themselves faced with incongruent situations occasionally. What does a doctor parent tell his child, who is burning up with fever, when he has to leave to attend someone else's child who is unwell? What does a doctor wife tell her husband when she leaves a dinner that they are hosting just as she has announced that dinner is served?

Practices have changed, technology has made its presence felt and yet the one thing that endures and what everyone is still looking for is the personal touch.

Those looking for medical help expect a doctor to 'be there'. A doctor is the person that one should be able to get in touch with anytime of the night or day, of course he can't 'go on a holiday', it's inconvenient if he has a personal emergency and heaven forbid, if he has a breakdown- then he is 'unreliable'.

Everyone wants a 'dedicated professional'. Professionals tend to put their personal lives on hold, set their targets or use the profession to run away from personal ghosts that maybe chasing them, thus making them 'dedicated'.

What seems to be forgotten is that the doctor is a human first- he eats, he sleeps, he laughs, he hurts, he cries. He has a family, friends, occasions and festivals that he needs to celebrate, holidays that are his due and also needs a 'balanced life' for his health like he advises everybody.

'On the Inside' is just such a story that explores the lives of four doctor friends outside their profession. 'Dedicated professionals' who in fact do not take time off to live but live in the time that they get off.

Prelude

I put the finishing touches to my face, getting ready for my date with Raghu, my love from medical college, in the hope that our date would actually happen, unlike the last time, a year ago.

Then, like today, I was dressing for my date when my phone rang.

It was Kajol, my friend, an airhostess, "Hi, do you know what's going on? People at the airport say that all roads from the airport into town have been cordoned off because of bomb blasts."

I live in a lane near Churchgate station and had been hearing sounds similar to gunshots for the past hour and thought it was a car backfiring or perhaps fireworks…

When I switched on my TV, I was stunned. Terrorists were on the rampage, taking hostages at Chabad House; firing at people in Leopold Café; the Taj and The Oberoi hotels were under siege; there was firing at the Chhatrapati Shivaji Rail Terminus; senior police officers had been injured and…

The lipstick fell out of my hands.

"Oh my God, Kajol! It's total mayhem here. It's best that you stay where you are; don't try to drive towards Colaba."

My thoughts had turned to Raghu, where was he? I tried calling him but the mobile network was jammed. TV was the only source of any news.

Raghu called three hours later. "Anuja, I had flown in just to meet you but it looks like our meeting is not to be. There seems to be chaos in the city. I am unable to leave the airport. Fortunately, the flights out of Mumbai are still leaving. Anuja…"

"I am listening," I said. "I am happy to just hear your voice. It makes a lot of sense to head back to Delhi now."

I was happy that he was safe, happy that he had flown in to Mumbai just to meet me but unhappy that we hadn't been able to meet.

The 'terrorist siege' went on for the next seventy-two hours.

Raghu called from Delhi later that day and every day for the next two days, till he flew back to Singapore.

Contents

G et up in the morning, get dressed, go to work, same faces, back home, TV dinner, clean up, watch the idiot box and then to bed. How boring...

Things were getting dull and monotonous. I seriously needed to get my life back. I smiled wryly, correction: I needed to get a life. Standing in my balcony, coffee mug in hand, staring at a small patch of sea visible between two buildings, the morning breeze in my face, I thought intently about my predicament, tucking a loose strand of hair behind my ear.

Smart, curvy, at forty plus, I had everything I could ask for. A flat in Mumbai, a car, a respectable bank balance... I was an upright member of society and I worked at a job that I actually enjoyed; why was I restless? Something was missing. I missed companionship. I missed having someone to share the tiny details of my day, a hug, a spontaneous laugh, impromptu plans... Dad and mom have always been there for me. But...

My thoughts went back to my six years at the College of Medicine (CM), Pune, which remain the most cherished and treasured years of my life. Being an only child, I had always led a sheltered existence. Since my parents had been stationed in Kolhapur during my medical years, med school had given me the chance to experience hostel life and an opportunity to explore and experiment, although still under strict 'distant' maternal supervision. The Spanish Inquisition happened over weekend phone calls; I had to give my mom a detailed lowdown on what I had been up to during the week. But well, the updates happened after "I had done it".

Sigh! I got nostalgic just thinking about the cutting chai (tea), the midnight bike rides, late night movies, college fests, inter-collegiate events, pranks, my first puff... The list of firsts was endless; there had never been a dull moment. Having an extremely close-knit group of friends who were equally tuned in had only enhanced the experience.

Our group, the famous four as we came to be known, was quite a mix. Although we were not all from the same batch we probably gravitated towards each other because of our similar diehard attitude. None of us understood the meaning of the word 'can't'. In fact, if someone said you couldn't do something, we made it a point to do it, just to prove them wrong. Be it converting the annual college fest into a super duper inter-collegiate five-day event 'SCORES' or revamping our one page, yearly college magazine 'Live it up' into a quarterly glossy.

Our college fest used to be a half-day event with a musical evening where an orchestra was paid to perform. That was till we decided to do something about it. Whatever happened to in-house talent? The first year we faced a lot of flak for our ideas. Many of our classmates were skeptical, but our enthusiasm was infectious and in spite of their reservations they turned up in large numbers to help. Just when we managed to get them all really into the mood our Dean became impossible. Our gang of four was subjected to a dose of, "The students are spending too much time on the preparations" and "Make sure all students have a minimum of 90 per cent attendance". I mean, come on, even the university asked for only 75 per cent attendance!

Within two years 'SCORES' was one of the most happening events, with as many as twenty medical colleges across the state participating in it. It was not a fest; it was a fiesta. We had quizzes, talent contests, Mister and Miss Score events and a musical bonanza. The best part of all was the sheer number of colleges participating in it. It was a lot of hard work but it was amazing. Late nights, last minute hitches, making makeshift arrangements was great fun. We enjoyed ourselves and actually made money from the event. We had been able to start a gymnasium and an all-night canteen on campus with what we raised. The Dean became our ardent supporter after we managed to rope in the Chief Minister to inaugurate 'SCORES' in the second year.

The honking of cars brought me back to the present. Sigh! Girl you'd better hurry or you will be late. As I was dressing I couldn't help wondering where and how the other three were. We had managed to keep in touch for a couple of years after college. Thereafter, being in different specialties, geographical locations, and life situations led us to drift apart. And surprisingly, although occasionally a common acquaintance would update you of someone's present location and situation, no direct communication materialised between us.

Looking back, I wonder why we did not reach out to each other earlier. What had stopped us? Were we worried about whether we would share the same bond now that we had had then; whether we would still connect; had things changed over the years? Sometimes, I guess you prefer to at least have memories.

"Well, Anuja," I had thought, "do you want to risk it and take a chance?" Considering my present mental state, I decided

I had nothing to lose and decided to launch a "get in touch with the others" campaign. It would give me something to do.

I put it on top of my to-do list as I rushed off to work. 'Work' is all I did. I was not a party animal, depended on the idiot box for my entertainment and honestly the only people I met were my hospital colleagues, patients and their relatives. I was leading such a sad life.

The week had been extremely busy and the weekend was on me before I realised it. The desire to find the others had taken a back seat.

Sunday morning saw me get out of bed with a rush of adrenaline. I had been motivating myself all week to get back to a healthy routine. I hit Marine Drive for a five-kilometre run. The fresh morning air and beautiful sunrise always pepped me up. Pink in the face after a refreshing run and feeling good about all things in general, I decided I needed to clean up my living space as well.

Hands on my hips, lips pursed, I surveyed my apartment. There were books and magazines wherever you looked, clothes draped over chairs and strewn all over the bed and washed clothes piled up on a chair that needed ironing. The house help had strict instructions not to touch personal items. I sighed as I looked around. Well, I only had myself to blame for the mess.

The house needed a thorough clean up. Feng Shui says that to allow positive energy to flow you need to declutter. I decided to go the whole hog and leave no stone unturned. This rare spring-cleaning drive had me pulling down old suitcases, files, drawers, and albums... That's when I chanced upon letters and photographs yellowed with age.

I went through the entire lot, reading the letters, looking at the photographs, and smiling to myself recalling the occasions. Pictures of dad and me parasailing in Pattaya. Mom hugging me, while I tried to struggle free. Wedding shots of my cousin's wedding. Oh! picture of the beer and barbecue on a full moon night on the beaches of Goa. There was a lively band, the girls had dressed in floral sarongs and the boys in shorts and T-shirts...That was the trip when Charles had caught me in the act of downing my first beer. There was also a picture of all of us grinning from ear-to-ear at the musical night of 'SCORES'... Before I realised it, it was past noon. I sighed. It was definitely time to find my friends.

As I picked myself off the floor and finally started putting things in place, I mused on how I would go about it. It shouldn't be difficult, I reasoned, what with the internet and social networking sites. Folks at work had been exchanging notes about how they had managed to trace so and so through these sites. There was only one hitch. I was "technologically challenged"; I only knew how to "Google Search" and access email accounts. Someone would have to help me figure out the social networking sites.

After a leisurely shower, I actually settled down with my laptop and a hot cup of coffee to try and get Google to help me figure out things for myself. Except that my cable guy had literally pulled the plug on me—no net! Silently cursing him, I went back to surfing the idiot box.

The time we take from thought to execution is directly proportional to the availability of time we can call your own. My heavy work schedule during the week kept me from active pursuit of this project. But I guess the cosmic connect (the Universe was conspiring to make this happen) was in place. A week later, I found an email nestling among the spam mails, an anaesthesia and critical conference notification and guess who was heading the scientific committee, Raghu. I couldn't help myself; I sent him a one-liner email."Hi stranger, remember me, Anuja?"

I was pleasantly surprised by an almost immediate reply, "Stranger hogi tu! Which part of the world are you in, what are you doing?"

We exchanged short warm emails; we still seemed to be on the same wavelength. Raghu was working out of Singapore. A couple of days later Raghu sent me a text, "Would the pretty lady join me for dinner on 26/11 at 9 pm at the Chopsticks."

I was ecstatic, I presumed Raghu was going to be in Mumbai for work and wanted to catch up. Well, so did I… want to catch up that is. My hands were already texting "Yes". I was still wary. I had neither met nor heard from Raghu in over two decades. But the heart still did a flip every time I thought of him. I had always carried a torch for him since our days in college. Had he known? Well, he knew I always considered him a dear friend, but Sonali? And then …I sighed and shrugged off the thoughts. Well, 26/11 was two days away, I smiled and hugged myself, something to look forward to. I really had a bad case of the butterflies.

The meeting never happened thanks to Kasab and party. It's been almost a year now. Raghu and I had been exchanging one-liners off and on during the last year. He had never been a great communicator; nothing had changed. He had this uncanny knack of falling off the radar, intermittently.

2

After connecting up with Raghu, the desire to trace the other two members of our group became more intense. I found myself thinking more and more about them.

A little help and advice later, bless the internet, I realised that the other two were only a 'mouse' click away. The Facebook friend-of-a-friend link helped me touch base with the others. We emailed each other. Everyone seemed happy to connect… yet for some reason the mails while being warm were distant. It was as if no one wanted to exchange any intimate details over the net. Things would be different once we all met face-to-face.

Anuja had decided that the face-to-face would happen. She decided to engineer the meeting that very week. Charles and Sonali were scheduled to be in Mumbai then and as for Raghu, she had persuaded him to fly in; they deserved a grand reunion party, she thought.

It was almost a year after 26/11. The Trident, at The Oberoi, had resurrected itself. It had become a symbol of the never-say- die spirit of Mumbai making it the perfect meeting ground for the reunion of the famous four. I had taken great pains to dress; we were meeting after twenty-five long years; seemed like eternity. I was finally going to meet Raghu.

As I put the finishing touches to my makeup, my palms were sweaty, my pulse was racing and my cheeks were a natural red. I was definitely nervous. Well, this time I had planned the perfect dinner, and no one was allowed to spoil this one. D-day was here. I took one last glance at the mirror, then turned and looked over my shoulder as I smoothed my black dress around my hips. The reflection revealed a woman of forty-plus... well, who looked in her mid-thirties; smart, fit, and with a great smile. A touch of Chanel No. 5, a single string of pearls around the neck, solitaires in the ears, and black stilts complemented my simple knee-length, A-line, black dress. I took a last twirl as I picked up my black and silver, embroidered clutch and headed out.

My cab dropped me off at the venue. Standing in line for my security check at the hotel (one couldn't even have a meal without being frisked, what a world we lived in), I stared out at the sea. Soft moonlight reflected off its gentle waves. It was beautiful. I took a deep breath as I entered. Well, here goes.

I glanced at my watch as I pushed my way into the restaurant. I was early. The maître d' saw me and bustled across the room to escort me to my table. The place was beautifully done up. It was perfect! It had to be. I had agonised over the venue and fussed over the plans for weeks.

I declined the maître d's offer for a drink; preferring to wait for the others. My thoughts strayed.

It seems like yesterday...

At seventeen, getting accepted to medical college leaves you with a sense of accomplishment and gratification. The bonds you forge and friendships that form then endure a lifetime.

My first day was firmly etched in my mind. Due to health reasons, I joined med school a month late. By then groups had already formed and their group dynamics were already in place. My first lecture was anatomy in the specimen hall.

Excited and apprehensive, dressed in jeans, a white kurti and Kolhapuri chappals, with two tight plaits neatly tucked away under the collar of my white knee length apron, books in hand, I walked towards an empty seat in the third row.

"Excuse me," I turned around to find a thin, lanky, mop-haired guy, with a non-descript face holding up a screw, "Yours I believe."

I took it out of his hand, turned it around just as seriously and then returned it with a sweet smile. Inwardly I was seething, "Wrong size, probably yours."

That was my introduction to Dr. Charles D' Souza, one of the famous four. Today's leading cardiothoracic surgeon of international repute. A success story in every way—socially, financially, and professionally. Settled in New York. He had made it to the cover of the Times a few years ago.

Charles had been born a natural surgeon. Fortunately for me, he had been on my dissection table and helped me overcome my aversion to the anatomy dissection sessions. When you have to sit across dismembered limbs and uncovered dead bodies (most of us encounter them for the first time) spread out on cold steel tables, formalin pervading every pore of your skin, day-in and day-out for over a year, you do start wondering whether you have made the right decision. I mean doctors are supposed to sit in sterile air-conditioned rooms in pristine white coats and dole out medical advice. What were we doing here cutting up dead bodies?

The first couple of days can be bad. I could not bring myself to eat after the dissection sessions. To make things worse, during the second week of joining college I returned to the girls' hostel late one evening and found a gentleman resembling the Don Juan on our dissection table sitting on the hostel stairs. I freaked out. I went to the library and made sure I was part of a small group when I returned. It turned out that the gentleman at the hostel was a local farmer who had come to deliver vegetables to the hostel kitchen!

Charles was my rock, he helped to make the dissection experience...well...more practical. In time the dissection process became only what it was supposed to be-a way to unravel the complexities of the human body. Thanks to that, in subsequent years, Forensic Medicine became quite my favourite and I actually enjoyed the autopsies.

As a matter of fact, all the members of the famous four were success stories today.

Dr. Sonali Dhillon, was a leading infertility specialist in India. Settled in Delhi, she had written and published three highly acclaimed books on the causes of infertility and its treatment. The books had been extremely well accepted and appreciated internationally.

Dr. Raghu Desai was a senior intensivist of world-repute. He was a globetrotter and had worked at hospitals of repute all over the world and was in the process of contemplating a shift back to India. An extremely committed and sought-after intensivist he was extremely active professionally and an excellent orator. No international intensive care conference was planned without him.

And then of course there's me, Dr. Anuja Deshpande, cardiothoracic anaesthesiologist. My claim to fame was that I worked with leading cardiothoracic surgeons at the Corporate Hospital, a premier institution of Mumbai. I dabbled in medical journalism and was a restless soul.

Another look at the watch revealed that I had been there just five minutes. Time really crawls when you are waiting. I chided myself, Anuja the watch hands are not going to move faster just because you are mooning over them. I was early.

I smiled and rubbed my hands in anticipation, I was finally going to meet Raghu. I sighed as I remembered him. It still sent shudders down my spine when I recall our last meeting. His face a mask, tearless, unseeing eyes, totally unaware of what was happening around him. The image still haunted me.

I went back to my thoughts.

3

Although from a traditional Punjabi family, Dr. Sonali Dhillon was a bohemian at heart. Her family owned acres and acres of land; they were both extremely rich and cultured. Very traditional and conservative yet forward-looking is how Sonali described them. Sonali was the eldest of three sisters and was her father's favourite. He had always supported her in all her endeavours and fulfilled her every desire. He had encouraged her pursuit of further studies. She was the opposite of her sisters: outgoing while they were docile, wanting to live life to the fullest while they were happy with what was offered, with a desire to be her own person recognised for her achievements while their only goal in life was to get good husbands and settle down.

"The bold and the beautiful" described her just right. Tall, fair, with a clear complexion and thick long silky black hair that extended below her waist, deep brown eyes that you could drown in and a figure to die for. And if that was not enough she was intelligent, vivacious and extremely focused. Some just have it all, sigh!

Except for the two guys who had issues with their own sexuality, every guy on campus fell in love with her the day she joined. No party was planned without her; no party happened without her. She was the life of the party with her energy and vivaciousness. Oh! And she was an accomplished singer. She was a batch senior to me. That we became friends was destiny.

It was my first day on labour room duty. No, not hard manual labour but delivery room duty that is part of medical training. Every medico goes through it, believe me, very few enjoy it.

The labour room was tucked away in a corner of the campus, probably so as not to scare other patients. It definitely sounded like a torture chamber when fully occupied. It was eerie at night. It was a small room of eight by ten feet with four, bare, peeling walls, a black clock on the wall, that went tick-tock loudly, a fan that groaned under the weight of the three blades as it moved but offered no relief from the heat, two light bulbs suspended by long wires swayed overhead. The instruments on the trolley glistened menacingly; in fact they definitely looked too big for any human use. The action stations were the four cold metal delivery tables that were arranged in parallel pairs against opposite walls.

It was around ten at night when I walked in. Two of the action stations were occupied. The occupants of the cold metal tables were writhing, breathing hard and pushing to encouraging shouts of "Dhakal, dhakal" (push, push), by the nursing staff. It definitely did not inspire confidence in a second year medical student who has never seen a delivery, forget conducted one before.

Dr. Sonali who was the senior on duty that day was perched on the only wooden table holding court while her two on-duty colleagues were seated on the only two steel chairs in the room. They all looked so... well... at home, chattering nineteen to a dozen and laughing as if they were in the canteen rather than the labour room. Sonali looked up and spotted me standing at the door, looking ready to flee. "Good you are here. Look it's late and we are all dying for a hot cuppa," looking at the women on the delivery tables, "It promises to be a long night. Hold fort. We'll be back in a while."

I looked at the two ladies. Dr. Sonali saw my panic and reassured me with a smile, "Don't worry, they both have at least an hour to go. We'll be back by then." This was said over her shoulder as she and her colleagues disappeared through the door.

I returned a watery smile to their disappearing backs. What I had not expected was that the two nursing staff would troop out after them as well.

Alone with two ladies pushing hard and breathing heavily, I folded my hands and sent up fervent prayers. God please help me. The clock ticked the minutes away ominously.

I picked up the case sheets on the table trying to make some sense out of them. I peered at the two ladies occasionally. Thankfully, the lady on table two had quietened down, she seemed to have fallen asleep. Now, if only the other one would also do the same till the reinforcements returned.

"Tick-tock, tick-tock..."

The lady on table one started panicking, I rushed to her side and started talking to her in a bid to calm her down. She was thrashing around. The delivery table seemed too small to accommodate her. God, don't let her fall off. "Look, just relax, I am Dr. Anuja, everything will be all right. Payal (that was the name on the file), I'll take care of you; everything will be all right." (Brave words, Anuja, hope you don't have to eat them my girl.)

My words did nothing to calm her. They did nothing to

calm me either. Probably my anxiety was being communicated to her rather than my reassuring words. Payal was in an extremely abusive mood. Her swears burnt my ears. She spared nobody; central to her abuse were her husband and mother-in-law.

She gripped my hand, the pressure increased progressively; her fingernails were digging into my palm. I wanted to scream as loudly as she was.

Hot, sweaty and swearing, Payal gave me a resigned look and said the words I was dreading, "I think I am about to deliver."

My hands turned cold and clammy. My heart was in my mouth. God, no! I looked around; there was no sign of help.

Taking two deep breaths, I tried to calm both her and myself.

I disentangled my now mangled, numb hand and positioned myself at the other end of the delivery table. I was breathing hard myself, I took two deep breaths to calm myself and tried to remember what they had taught us in the theory class. Oh no, a black head was staring back at me. Oh my God! She was crowning, it was here.

The very next moment, in one smooth slow motion, something glistening, slimy and slippery was coming my way. I had not even had time to wear my gloves. Just as I managed to position myself like a wicket-keeper on the cricket field, something slid into my hands. God, it almost slipped out. I somehow, managed to hang on to it by its leg. Remembering some theory from my gynaecology/obstetric class, I held it upside down. Yippee, the baby bawled without any assistance.

From, the corner of my eye, I saw my angels of mercy, the

senior nursing staff troop in. One look was enough for them to size up the situation.

"Dr. Anuja, hand me the baby."

Just as I thankfully handed over the baby they said, "Dr. Anuja, watch out the second one is on the way."

Second one? Glad she warned me, I had just enough time to reposition myself before another slippery slimy thing came my way. Being more experienced now, I did a better job of hanging on.

I was sweating, my heart was galloping, I was covered in amniotic fluid and stinking, but then again, I had just delivered twins!

At that moment Dr. Sonali entered with her colleagues. They took one look at the scene and couldn't stop laughing. Leaving the tying and cutting of the umbilical cord to the staff, I glowered at them and literally stomped off angry and stinky. And not a moment too soon, the lady on table two had started stirring…

That was the day I knew what I did not want to become—an obstetrician/ gynaecologist and also the day that I befriended Dr. Sonali.

The more I came to know her the more I learned to love her. There were no rules in her book. She was down-to-earth and caring. She had all the guys eating out of her hand. The only one that bothered me was Dr. Raghu. He talked about her every time we were together. It had really started to get to me; didn't the guy realize I had, well feelings for him? At one point in time I thought she was also serious about Raghu. I tried asking her and got a tongue in cheek, "Dr. Raghu is a nice guy and someone, I could get serious about."

Then there was also, Dr. Shubham Mehra, the college heartthrob, two years her senior.

"Sonali, Dr. Mehra can't take his eyes off you, what's up?"

'That's true for all the guys! He's just another one.'

We had a grand party on the last day of her internship. Having decided on obs/gynae as her area of interest she had decided to accept a residency in the obs /gynae department of a hospital at Delhi, nearer home as she said. I was really going to miss her. We stayed in touch for a while.

She was a poor letter writer. Her communication was infrequent, and reduced to a trickle as time wore on. Her last letter had read:

Dear Anuja,

Guess what, Charles has also signed up for his surgical training here. It's good to have an old friend around.

Love Sonali.

Why she had wasted money on an inland letter, when what she wanted to say would have fit behind a postage stamp was beyond me.

Through common acquaintances, I later learnt that she had completed her training in gynaecology with flying colours. Dr. Charles on the other hand, dropped off my radar thereafter. What I knew was pieced together from all his media stories considering how successful he was.

I was really looking forward to meeting all of them, especially Raghu.

4

Raghu was my batch mate. Tall and smart; he loved his books and music. He was well informed and oh, he was handsome in a quiet sort of way. He had thick black hair, black eyes, side burns and was always clean-shaven. He was a non-smoker and a family man.

Raghu was an only son. His father, Satyendra Desai, came from a family of cloth merchants. They dealt in both stitched and unstitched materials. He had a brother named Rajendra. Satyendra was the younger of the two. Rajendra had taken charge of the family at a young age and never married. The family had run an extremely successful joint business. They had four huge outlets all over town. Raghu had been brought up in the lap of luxury. He had literally been born with a silver spoon. Being the only child in the family he was totally pampered, his every wish was fulfilled before it was expressed.

The Desai family was very patriarchal. The eldest brother led and the family followed, no questions asked; they were extremely close-knit. However, all happy stories have a way of going wrong. It was the time of the real estate and share market boom; the age of Harshad Mehta. In a bid to take advantage of the market situation and make some fast money Rajendra decided to diversify and got into a partnership for a supposedly roaring real estate business. In spite of his business acumen and experience the partners took him to the cleaners, the business folded and Rajendra found that he had signed all the loan papers as sole guarantor for the business. He was left holding the losses, while the partners walked away with the money and profits. To get out of the mess, he had to sell the cloth business. First the shops went, then the factory and finally even the ancestral house.

Cheated out of everything, the Desai family had been reduced to leading a hand-to-mouth existence. More than the financial loss it was having the family name dragged through mud that got to the brothers. Both of them took it very hard; they died of broken hearts within months of each other. There were rumours that Raghu's father had actually committed suicide. He had gone to bed one night and did not wake up the next morning. They had apparently found sleeping pills in his system on post mortem. The insurance company had refused to pay up. Raghu had been fourteen.

Raghu was forced to grow up overnight. He and his mother moved into a one-room set-up in a chawl. His mother, Maya, refused to let Raghu quit school. She started doing odd jobs. She put together a dabba (tiffin) service and also took orders for homemade pickles and papads. She made sure that by the time Raghu entered medical college on a scholarship, they had moved into a small, independent, one bedroom house with a small kitchen. Raghu was devoted to his mother.

Raghu's father had arranged his son's marriage as a child with his friend's daughter Veena, who was also an only child. Veena lost her parents in a car crash at the age of seventeen. The family had been returning after a visit to Shirdi. A huge trailer jumped the road divider on the Mumbai-Nashik Highway and hit the Matador they were travelling in head on. Veena had been in the car but surprisingly had escaped with few bruises and a mild concussion. Her mother had actually thrown herself over Veena at the time of the crash. She had stayed there pinned under her mother for some time before the rescue team arrived. A sweet, quiet girl she had been extremely traumatised by the accident and had been informed of her parent's death only after a month. It devastated her.

Raghu's mother had come to her rescue and brought her home. Having a young girl living with them, that too one betrothed to her son, set tongues wagging. So Raghu's mother prevailed upon him to marry, albeit reluctantly, even before finishing his medical graduation. The day Veena turned eighteen the two were wed in a simple but beautiful ceremony.

Raghu was the only one who married in his final year of medicine. Though his was an arranged marriage, he had come to love his wife.

Veena, his wife, was a real gentle soul. She had studied only up to the eighth standard. She was a very nice person and a true homemaker. She adored her widowed mother-in-law and bent over backwards to look after her. She managed the house as well as helped her mother-in-law in her business. An ideal wife; she worshipped the ground that Raghu walked on. He in turn really looked after her, a real made-for-each other couple. I used to tell Sonali jokingly, "Maybe we need to look at the boys our parents want us to meet; an arranged marriage may not be such a bad idea." To which her standard remark was, "UGH!"

Veena, knew the way to our hearts as well. The number of times she sent us packed biryani and sandesh enough to feed an army—the intern army—was amazing.

Raghu ensured that he enjoyed all the privileges of being the only "taken guy" in the batch. We covered for him on all holidays, all festivals, and well whenever he decided he needed time with his wife. He was blessed with a son on the last day of our internship and was ecstatic!

Raghu signed up for his MD Anaesthesiology and also took up a locum Chief Medical Officer post to supplement his income.

I had always had a soft corner for Raghu and had well hoped, he felt 'something'. That changed once he got married. From my side the torch never went out. Raghu was always caring; but whether he had any romantic feelings for me I never knew.

Yet I found our proximity distressing at times. After my internship I applied for and got accepted into a residency programme in Anaesthesiology in Mumbai so I moved on.

5

I shook myself out of my reverie. It was finally nine o'clock. The others would be here any moment now.

Yes, the meeting of the famous four. I rubbed my hands in anticipation, a wicked smile on my face; the best part of the evening was that the others did not know that it was to be a reunion night. Each of them believed that they would be dining with me alone. I couldn't wait to see the look on their faces.

Two decades ago, communication was not what it is today. There was no instant messaging or emails; letters took ages to reach and telegrams were harbingers of misery mostly. A waiting list of two to three years for a telephone connection ensured that only the privileged few had a contact number. Even a telephone connection did not mean you were well-connected. You couldn't just decide to make a call. For a long distance STD call the two concerned parties needed to fix up a day and time well in advance. A trunk call as it was called then, would be booked; one could pay extra for a "lightning" call. The receiver had to ensure that he was available near the nearest decided telephone, the neighbour's home or the matron's office for the three-minute pleasure of talking to a loved one.

In fact, I still remember that the local students in the hostel who enjoyed the privilege of getting home-cooked dabbas from home, used the dabbas as a way of communicating with their family. The letters and messages that travelled back and forth with the dabba kept them updated on what was happening at home.

Cumbersome communication channels are probably the only reason that we lost touch with each other in the first place. If we had had Facebook, Twitter, and all the other modes of keeping in touch that are available today, our life stories would probably have been different. We would have been updating our status and uploading pictures on the move. As the saying goes, "Har friend jaroori hain" (every friend is important).

Never mind. At least we have it all today. It was the net, which had finally helped me track down my long lost friends.

I looked up to see Sonali walk in as ethereal and beautiful as ever, she had not changed. Her blue off-shoulder dress accentuated her long neck, which was adorned with a pretty diamond studded choker. As the maître d' escorted her to the table, every head in the room turned to follow her; even the women couldn't help but stare. Gorgeous as ever, she drew a reaction from everyone. The men being smitten by her was a given but I think even the women either fell in love with her or envied her.

I stood up as she neared the table. We fell into each other's arms, we hugged, we cried, we laughed. As we drew apart I saw the questioning look in Sonali's eyes. Did I remember our last meeting?

Twenty years, it seems like yesterday.

I had completed my MD Anaesthesiology at the Government Medical College in Mumbai. Not having decided on my further course of action, I had joined Sudha Private Hospital as a post MD senior registrar. On that fateful day

I found myself covering the gynae/obs list as my consultant was delayed. After my experience with the twins, I still hated the specialty. But rota is rota. The gynaecological practice at Sudha was roaring.

I groaned as I looked at the list for the day-four cesarean sections and four dilation and curettage/MTP (medical termination of pregnancy) procedures. Why people had stopped delivering normally was beyond me. It seems that birth control does not work in this country and on the other hand promiscuity is increasing. Haven't people heard of condoms at least? More than half of the people undergoing MTPs were unmarried teenagers. "Well, their indiscretion was our business, literally."

How I hated the smell of the gynaecology operating theatre. "Anuja you better decide what you want to do in life, and get on with it." Thus castigating myself, I got down to work. Checking the anaesthesia machine and preparing drugs.

I was still cursing myself when Dr. Asha the gynaecologist, whose list I was to do called me aside.

"Anuja we'll start with Manju. She's in a bad state. Her family is unaware of her condition and I am doing this as a personal favour to her aunt, Saroj, who is my friend. Take care of her."

Wondering at all the mystery, I shrugged my shoulders. Another MTP, big deal. First you mess around and then want someone to clean it up. My frustration at having to do the list was getting to me.

Manju was wheeled in and shifted on to the operating table.

I was loading my anaesthetics and had my back to her.

"Hi Manju, I am your anaesthesiologist. Just relax we'll take good care of you. Do you have any medical…"

My voice trailed off because as I turned around I saw Sonali on my table. I blinked, looking at her in complete disbelief.

"Manju…?"

I don't know who was more surprised or shocked. "Sonali, what…"

She looked away distressed. Sonali broke down. She refused to look at me. I realised I was not going to get any answers to the many questions I had.

"Are you sure, do you know what you are doing?"

The moment I uttered the words I realised how stupid I sounded. Medically she knew, personally she would not be here if she had not decided to. Sonali was stubborn; you could never make her do what she did not want to.

She was trembling like a leaf but determined to continue. I felt like grabbing her by the shoulders and shaking her hard.

Realising that she was already distressed, I decided to hold my counsel and not be judgmental.

Resigned, I restricted my questioning to her medical history, which she condescended to answer in monosyllables.

"Are you hypertensive?" "No".

"Are you diabetic?" "No."

"Any loose teeth?"

What was I thinking? Sonali had a perfect thirty-two. The fact was I was not thinking, I was questioning by rote.

"No".

"Any known allergies?"

"No".

"Any previous anaesthesia experience for any minor or major procedures?"

That got me a look that said, "Et tu Brutus!"

"Closed reduction right forearm fracture, short GA, uneventful." Crisp, to the point, although the voice was unsteady.

How well I remember the right forearm fracture that Sonali had sustained trying to scale the drainpipe to our hostel room after a late night movie.

Our hostel was a double-storey building. The curfew time was 9 pm. At eighteen and nineteen we thought we were adult enough to stay out later than that. What was a late night movie? The hostel girls were all in on the trick and we covered for each other when needed. We would stuff the pillows under the blankets on the bed before taking off, just in case the matron did surprise checks.

Sonali broke her arm as we lowered ourselves onto the terrace; she fell on her hand which she had extended to break her fall. She was in pain, and one look at the swelling and we knew we had no choice but to inform someone. We woke up the matron and told her Sonali had slipped in the loo. She had surveyed our situation with interest; we stood in front of her dressed in jeans, t-shirts and sandals, it was well past midnight and one of us had a broken arm. She had been sporting enough to keep quiet. Sonali was her favourite. The matron had fussed over Sonali, taken her to the casualty ward, got the X-ray done, got her hand plastered and given her a hot cup of milk with her medication. I only got a look that said, "You should have known better". Though for a couple of months after that, the matron did regular rounds sharp at nine and checked under 'suspect' blankets.

I don't know who exploited the fact that Sonali had sustained a fracture more, she or the boys. "Let me carry your books. "Can I hold your plate while you eat?" "Can I give you a lift?" I rolled my eyes each time. Come on she had a fractured hand not a foot. Sonali was everyone's sweetheart.

Dr. Asha came in and all further conversation was impossible. The procedure was uneventful.

Although I knew Sonali did not want to see me, I couldn't help myself; I went looking for her after my list.

Her aunt had discharged her and taken her home almost immediately after the procedure. No forwarding address, without so much as a by your leave.

I did not know whether I was sad or mad.

Today all that did not seem important. I was just so happy to see her. Sonali's hug seemed to echo my feelings. We were just pulling apart when I sensed 'HIM'.

6

I felt his presence. Yes, Raghu had just walked in. He looked amazing. Except for the head full of salt and pepper that really suited him, he hadn't changed. Dressed in a light blue full-sleeved shirt, black well-cut trousers and black polished shoes, he looked handsome. The side burns had gone... my heart did a somersault; a usual response to his being near me, nothing had changed. Damn him. He had always had that effect on me and yet he had never known, sigh! My well-kept secret. I had cried buckets the day he had announced his engagement and cried even more the day he married.

I seemed to be doing flashbacks on first sighting my friends. A few years after my MD, coming to terms with my feelings and gathering a little confidence, I had gone back to look up Raghu. It was too late, he had moved away without a forwarding address. I couldn't believe that he was now actually in the same room as me. Finally.

Raghu was looking at us. It was good to see him. I was grinning from ear to ear. Raghu stopped, our eyes locked across the room. He almost ran the distance and hugged both Sonali and me. I savoured the moment. But wait, it seemed that Sonali got a longer hug than me. No, just my imagination, I guess. We were all hugging, laughing, and crying, all at the same time.

Realising that every eye in the restaurant was on us, we pulled ourselves apart and took our seats, as expected of dignified, upstanding medical consultants of society.

Raghu looked at both of us, "You girls just look great. It's as if the years in between never happened."

Then looking suspiciously at me he said, "Tell me Charles is not coming as well, is he?"

For some reason, I turned sideways to look at Sonali. The moment she heard Charles' name she turned white as sheet, the colour drained from her face.

"Well…"

I nodded with a quiet smile, "Guilty as charged."

"Trust Anuja to do the unexpected. I should have smelt a rat when she was so insistent that I come in. I am glad I did. Well, I guess you know what a rough time Charles has been through."

"Rough time and Charles?" Sonali and I chorused.

Charles, an orphan who had been raised by his bachelor uncle of modest means, always talked of all the things he wanted to possess-mansions, cars, seven star holidays, name, fame, and pots and pots of money, not necessarily in that order. He had achieved it all, actually lived his dreams. He had been determined to make life compensate for everything he felt it had denied him as a child.

"Raghu, give me a break. Charles is a success story few can even dream about. He owns the world. Mansions in New York, Manhattan and Chicago. He even owns some exotic Greek island, a yacht and a fleet of cars…He breakfasts with presidents, lunches with prime ministers, and dines with Hollywood stars. He is a jet-setting, high-flying cardiac surgeon with an excellent reputation."

"I mean he's the cover story and the page three guy. Rough time...eh?"

Raghu looked thoughtful, "Anuja, since when have you started judging success by the size of cheque books.

"I still remember what you used to tell Charles, 'I need money to get myself treated if I suffer from a heart attack, but money cannot prevent a heart attack', right?"

"Come on, I have realised that if the cheque book is big enough, all problems become small. The size of a problem is inversely proportional to the size of a cheque book."

Raghu gave me a funny look while signaling the waiter to take our drinks and order starters. He ordered a whisky for himself and Bloody Marys for us. Charles had not yet put in an appearance. The drinks were prompt in their arrival as were the lovely roasted tiger prawns.

Raghu gave both of us a warm smile and bowed his head as we raised our drinks to make a toast, "To the two most beautiful women in the world, and the most handsome man around." Just to tease him, I turned my head to look around the room as though to search for the handsome guy he was talking about. Raghu laughed. Oh Raghu! Things hadn't changed; my heart was going all funny on me. "Anuja, get a grip on yourself," I thought to myself.

"Seriously girls, Charles has been through a lot." Raghu had a somber look on his face as he said it.

"I met Charles last year. I had travelled to New York for a conference and spent an evening with him. He owns a ten bedroom, old renovated mansion with almost twenty acres of landscaped lands about an hour's drive from New York not to mention a penthouse in the middle of New York. It had surprised me that he did not ask me to stay with him, in fact he did not even invite me home to the mansion.

"Although, he was definitely happy when I called him. The only thing he kept repeating was, 'I can be myself when I am with you'. Believe it or not we went to a bar for dinner. He got real emotional after a drink or two and silent Charles began to talk. It was as if years of suppressed emotions broke out. He talked of college times. In fact he mentioned both of you a couple of times."

He reached for Sonali's hand absentmindedly and held it. Sonali seemed to be getting uncomfortable, as Charles' story progressed. Well, I was getting uncomfortable myself. I was unable to comprehend the undercurrents that were flowing between Raghu and Sonali.

"As you know, he wrote his own success story. He left Delhi (looking at Sonali) after he got his fellowship in cardiothoracic surgery in Chicago. He moved to the States and proved himself academically.

"Always ambitious, he married the Chief 's daughter, Victoria. His father-in-law Dr. Alex Cunningham adored Charles. Dr. Alex was on the hospital's Board of Directors, well-connected socially and politically and not to forget the family fortunes. Victoria was his only daughter.

"The marriage started off like a fairy tale. Charles was convinced that he was in love with Victoria. All the

Cunningham contacts opened up doors for Charles, socially and professionally. He got 'accepted'. In the very first year of marriage Charles and Victoria were blessed with a son, Alex II, named after his father- in-law.

"Long hours at work and his anxiety to get bigger, faster took a toll on the fairy tale wedding. Victoria had always been a social butterfly; parties were her existence. Over time Victoria became an alcoholic. She was in and out of rehab.

"Alex II was an extremely intelligent and studious child. He was also an excellent sportsman. Apparently Charles had found out that Alex had started doing drugs and it was as if his whole world had crashed. He was in extreme depression and was blaming himself for the state his family was in. Charles went into a shell, stopped socialising, and began spending more time in hospital. He had almost become a recluse.

"He was extremely emotional when he spoke of Alex II. Alex II was refusing to meet him half way. Alex was refusing to talk to Charles unless he and Victoria sat down with him together. The fact that Victoria and he were barely on talking terms was not helping. He was at his wits end about what to do.

"That evening he really opened up to me. But, thereafter Charles has refused to even answer my calls. I have been trying to reach him especially after the reports started appearing in the media."

Total silence descended after this disclosure. The media had been having a field day. Charles had maintained a stoic public silence. Poor Charles, everything and yet nothing...

Raghu turned to Sonali, as he released her hand and picked up his glass, "When is the last time you spoke to Charles?"

Sonali was still pale. She seemed uncomfortable with the question. "Well, not after Delhi, actually. I bumped into him a couple of times when I was touring for my lecture series, but well, he preferred to behave as if I did not exist. In fact, on one occasion, when a colleague tried to formally introduce us, he actually turned away and walked off."

The minutes ticked by. Sonali seemed disturbed. Raghu, was well, he was holding her hand again. I was flummoxed. Raghu seemed to be very interested in Sonali. Charles did not want to acknowledge that Sonali existed. What was I missing? We had all got lost in our own thoughts after Raghu's disclosure and not registered Charles' entry and progress towards our table. He was looming large over us before we realised.

"Well, well, well, what do we have here? I thought this was to be a quiet dinner for two with an old friend, seems like I walked into a party." Charles was at the table looking daggers at me. He was fuming.

Even at that moment, I couldn't help notice that the mop haired man with a non-descript face, had transformed into an elegantly coiffured, designer labelled, confident, handsome man with chiselled features and probably a six-pack, who wore his after-shave musk with attitude.

Charles gave Sonali a disgusted look before turning on his heel and staging a walkout. The whole episode barely lasted seconds. Once again we were the centre of attraction. Sonali, looked wild and shaken and gave me an apologetic look as she followed Charles out. Raghu got up as if to follow her; but seemed to change his mind.

It was extremely embarrassing. Me sitting and Raghu half standing, watching the other two walk off. Raghu shrugged, shook his head and sat down. I was red in the face. I wish I had not given into my enthusiasm and arranged the surprise that seemed to have somehow gone horribly wrong. Probably feeling sorry for me, and realising that I was on the verge of tears, Raghu gently covered my hand with his and stroked it.

With a tender look, he held my hand, "Looks like it's going to be a party for two after all, a candle light dinner with a lovely lady." Ever caring Raghu. I gave him a watery smile. We settled down with our drinks. I picked up my Bloody Mary and tapped my glass. I was a little nervous.

"So tell me Anuja, how have you been, where have you been, how has life been treating you? Husband? Kids? You refuse to reveal any details in your one-liners… And actually two-minute phone chats. It's as if you were enticing us to come, find out more…"

"Oh no, you first. You, have been the one who has literally been around the world having an exciting time. Tell me the details. How has life been treating you?"

7

I remembered Raghu as I had seen him last. It had been from a distance and I had not had it in me to go speak to him.

In the first year of his residency, Raghu had planned to celebrate his son's first Diwali with a bang. He promised to take his mother, Veena and Raj (his son) to his maternal cousin's place on Bhau Bhij day. An entire day of family celebrations had been planned. A last minute rota change saw Raghu in the Casualty Ward at 8 am instead of at the breakfast feast he had planned.

Raghu was an exceptionally conscientious doctor and took his duties very seriously, but that day he was extremely upset at the unfair rota change. The Dean's son who was to have been on call had some urgent work, which really means that he wanted to enjoy a long Diwali weekend. To add to his woes, everybody, except the medical staff seemed to have decided to spend their Diwali at the hospital casualty. The flow of patients refused to stem. Cracker related injuries, food poisoning because of bad quality sweet meats, asthmatics reacting to the firecracker smoke, the usual aches and pains, attacks of appendicitis, intestinal perforations… By 2 pm Raghu was really frustrated. His two o' clock reliever failed to turn up. Raghu had really been looking forward to the weekend and was cursing his luck.

By 3 pm the patient flow had finally reduced to a trickle, but there was no reliever in sight, no messages from anyone either. By now a normally cool Raghu was seething, he'd had enough. He told the medical attendant to hold any further patients for his reliever. Taking off his white coat, scooping his stethoscope off the table, Raghu rushed out of the casualty ward.

On his way out, he bumped into a man with blood splattered on his shirt; who caught him by the arm. "Doctor Saheb please wait, there is an accident case coming."

Raghu hesitated momentarily, and then realising that a medicolegal case would take ages to sort out had brushed the man off. He had been abrupt and said, "My reliever will do the needful," jumped on to his Bajaj scooter and pushed off.

On his way he passed a badly smashed up auto lying on its side which had been rammed into by a loaded truck. These were possibly the accident victims being brought into casualty. The scene was quite gruesome. It was unlikely that those in the auto had made it. Poor souls, it was not much of a festival day for them. He silently prayed for them and sent up a thank you prayer for his own family and accelerated. The needles on the watch were pushing four. He needed to get home fast.

I could see Raghu was reliving the day. As he narrated the events I could actually visualise them unraveling scene by scene.

Raghu putting his scooter hurriedly on the stand, helmet in hand ran into the house calling out, "Veena, I'm back let's go."

His mother came out, "Raghu, what are you doing here? Veena and Raj left around one-thirty, and they planned to pick you up on the way. I had some last minute orders that I had to finish and promised to join you all later."

Raghu stopped in his tracks. It was just half an hour from the house to the hospital. It was pushing four-thirty now. They had been gone over three hours. Where were they?

"They probably met someone on the way. It is Diwali you know, they are both very popular in the neighbourhood." Raghu's mother wiped her hands on a napkin and patted his hand reassuring him.

Raghu scoured the neighbourhood after calling up his cousin, Saket, only to learn that Veena and Raj had not reached. Then commenced a long search. Every possible relative and friend was called upon or where possible phoned.

The search ended three hours later in the morgue. A truck had hit the auto rickshaw in which Veena and Raj had been travelling. They were the accident victims that Raghu had refused to wait and attend to.

Raghu never recovered from the tragedy. He kept reliving the way he had refused to wait at the casualty and then the sight of the mangled auto he had passed on the way home. He became a zombie, he refused to eat, and he couldn't sleep. Every time he tried he would wake up drenched in cold sweat, the sight of the mangled auto rickshaw, visions of Veena and Raj reaching out to him for help haunted him. He couldn't cry.

From the moment that Raghu realised what had happened, he stopped living. He became a permanent fixture in the hospital. He was everybody's reliever, working round the clock in a bid to bury his ghosts.

His mother, the poor lady, died of a broken heart within six months. She blamed herself for what had happened and wished she had accompanied Veena and Raj. His mother's death was like the proverbial last straw. Raghu created this huge emotional fortress around himself. It was as if he had inured himself from responding humanly. Raghu completed his postgraduate degree and took to travelling like a nomad. Never stopping long enough to form relationships. Only work drove him. This rolling stone was an acclaimed intensivist today.

We both exchanged a look that said it all.

After a pause he said, "Anuja, it was probably my restlessness, my devils that were chasing me. I wanted to be rid of them"

"Have you managed to slay your dragons?"

Raghu ran a hand through his hair. He looked so vulnerable in that one moment. "I am at least able to talk about it now. Anuja, even today, the ifs and buts of that day haunt me—IF I had waited, IF they had not left without me...The most difficult thing to do in life is to live with yourself.

"I tried everything, I worked till I was ready to drop, submerged myself in research, published papers and won accolades. Every success was empty. Even the running did not help. You can run away from situations, from places but how do you run away from yourself?"

Raghu took a deep breath and let out a sigh. There was a minute's silence as Raghu twirled the contents of his glass, looking into its depths as if it held the answers. He gave me a weak smile as he looked up and continued.

"It really took a patient of mine to start healing me at least enough to develop a scar. It was a couple of years later, after I had joined the Singapore Hospital Intensive Care Unit (ICU) as a junior consultant. I met Sonia, a cute, cherubic five-year-old, blue-eyed girl with blonde hair tied into two side fountains, who had a smile that could melt the coldest of hearts. She would get admitted for regular blood transfusions for her leukemia. The ICU would light up every time she came in.

"I have never been able to figure out why all children with cancer actually resemble angels. They all look so, well, pink cheeked, radiant and cute. Probably in a way they are the angels who are sent for short spells with the sole purpose of teaching people how to appreciate life and be better people.

"Well, Sonia took a shine to me and insisted that only I should take her intravenous line each time. She refused to let anyone else touch her. I resisted initially, but to no avail." A sad smile came on as he said it.

"It became a regular happening. The moment Sonia came in to hospital, no matter what, I would be informed. In fact her dad always called ahead and made sure I was around when they came in. I always fought off anybody who came close to me till then. She got through; I started spending as much time as I could with her between rounds and patients. I started calling her my sweetheart. She was mature beyond her years. She was the angel that taught me to smile again. She insisted on calling me Dr. Rag.

"She would keep saying, 'Dr. Rag, why are you such a sour puss? God gave us speech so we could communicate, God gave us lips so we could smile, God is gonna be very upset if you don't use his gifts right.' This was initially when I answered all her chatter with 'uhs and ahs'.

"Each time Sonia got admitted she made sure she came in armed with every possible pj (poor joke) available and all the latest news in the world of music and fashion. A smile on my face was the gratification she looked for; it rewarded all her efforts.

"I still remember her mischievous grin as she said, 'Dr. Rag you look so handsome when you smile. You know I think you need to get yourself a girlfriend. After I am gone of course; right now you are taken.'

"A year from our first meeting Sonia was brought in with septicemia from which she never recovered. 'Dr. Rag, you know you are wonderful. I will tell God to take special care of you when I meet him', was the last thing she said to me, before I put her on the ventilator."

Raghu lapsed into silence. Shaking himself mentally he continued, "Her death affected me real bad. It was as if everyone that I came to care for left me. What Sonia made me realise was that no matter what our own personal tragedies, you can still be a light in someone else's life.

"Anuja, I have decided to stop running, I'm tired now. I have been a rolling stone. You can run from situations, you can run from people," a pause, then a sigh, "you can't run from your shadows; they follow you. Yourself you have to learn to live with. It's taken me this long to admit it."

Mentally shaking himself Raghu leaned forward as if to share a secret, "Incidentally, I am seriously contemplating a move to Mumbai. The new group, the Forum Hospital, opening at Mira road, wants me to join as the Head of their Critical Care unit. They have visions of starting an air ambulance and putting together a real state-of-the-art Emergency and Trauma Care Centre. They want me to help plan and execute the project." He leaned back to see my reaction better.

"New challenges, means more work and less time to yourself Raghu I know you. Still running."

But wait, Raghu was talking of moving to Mumbai... Yippee... Hope Raghu couldn't read my mind.

"Forum Hospital..." "Yeah."

I had been invited by them to join as the Chief Cardiothoracic Anaesthesiologist. I was to reply next week. I was in a comfort zone at work presently and had been dithering. Now I had food for thought, reasons to seriously realign my "Why I shouldn't" in favour of "Why I must". But for now I kept my counsel and did not mention it to Raghu.

The remainder of the evening was a blur. We danced a little, laughed a lot and I guess I definitely got drunk. I have vague memories of Raghu dropping me off home.

8

And me? Dr. Anuja Deshpande. I belong to a simple, middleclass, business Maharashtrian family, technically, well… Mom is a Punjabi and Dad is a Maharashtrian. As an only child, I generally got my way with them, although they ensured that I wasn't spoilt. In fact I was an extremely considerate, obedient, loving, and accommodating girl till the age of fourteen. Thereafter, the hormones broke and it was rebellion time.

I would attend traditional family weddings in my jeans, kurti, and Kolhapuri chappals (my trademark gear those days), much to my mother's consternation. The lack of ornaments or makeup did not help matters. "What is more important, my being there or what I am wearing?" was my logic that was supposed to explain my behaviour. Poor mom. Especially with her Punjabi background, the importance of following a dress code was firmly ingrained in her. A touch of kajol (eyeliner) and lipstick were the least you could do. Pretty dresses, matching footwear and latest styles were definitely desirable.

Considering my "hybrid" background, which according to my aunts did not augur well for my matrimonial prospects, my behaviour only compounded the problem.

My saving grace was that I loved books, studied hard and was career oriented. Standing at 5ft 5", slightly (well, okay moderately) overweight, two tight plaits, and what is called a unibrow (you know, eyebrows that run from one end to the other without a break), wearing my trademark gear, carrying a Santiniketan cloth bag, wearing thick, round, black, framed spectacles (that I did not need but insisted on wearing because it makes you look more serious you know) that covered my fair, light-brown eyes, describes me perfectly at seventeen. Not too bad to look at if I may say so myself.

College was a disaster. I realised real early that I was a societal misfit; in every way I was wired differently. It was not as if I wanted to be different, or did not want to belong, so to say. Somehow makeup and boys were just not the centre of my universe even as a teenager. "Waste of time," is what I thought of that stuff. It was all right as a conversation starter, but I couldn't agonise about "Ooh that pretty pink lipstick" that someone was wearing, or the "Lovely earrings" and then discuss earring intricacies in considerable depth. Discussions about boys were the pits! Just because you find a guy cute you expect him to come running after you? I mean you did not even know whether the guy knew you existed, then you agonised about all the other girls he could possibly be interested in and then try to find corny lines and ways to "just bump into them". First you want to get them interested then when he asks you for a cup of coffee you refuse and then gloat about how you turned him down. Give me a break; there are better ways of spending one's life.

In trying to find new distractions I joined the Medical National Cadet Corps (NCC) because they were running a parasailing course. I will never forget the conversation I had with mom one weekend. My "Guess what, I have been parasailing this week," was met with pin-drop silence from the other end. A minute later (I thought we had been disconnected), the only response I got was, "What's broken?" My mother supported my father's oft expressed belief that if the good Lord had not joined all my body parts so well I would have been a missing many by now.

In a bid to conform, I tried to do a girly thing, probably certain comments about my lack of feminine characteristics by the opposite sex; especially the "ice maiden" comment might have triggered it. I participated in the Miss Pune contest and actually made it to the last five without much effort. The last question had me seething. I was asked to comment on "The pen is (penis is how the guy who was questioning phrased it. I couldn't stand the smug grin on his face as he said it) mightier than the sword". That was the last straw, talk about being an MCP (male chauvinist pig). That was my first and last tryst with femininity so to speak. Although it did do the trick, my reputation improved. My college mates were amazed at the transformation I could bring about when I so desired. I became the talk of the college for a while and actually got propositioned by a couple of guys over a couple of months. In fact one of them sent his parents over to our house with a marriage proposal; that helped lay my insecurities to rest.

It took a while for me to accept myself and find a group which allowed me to be myself. The famous four helped me settle in, although we too agreed to disagree over things.

Philosophy was my calling. Ferreting out the meaning of life and existence… Material things were immaterial…Karma was important. The Karma theory had been a big bone of contention between Charles and me throughout medical school. I talked philosophy; he talked everything material. Yet, we enjoyed healthy discussions all the same. No one wanted to back off, each made every effort to convert the other. Sonali and Raghu would sit back and enjoy the banter, while refusing to take sides; they continuously added fuel to fire.

I did not see eye to eye on different issues with various people. I had no intentions of getting married—a big bone of contention with my mom.

My poor mom tried cajoling, convincing and scolding in a bid to knock some sense into me. "It is young blood, you can't spend your life alone, and you need someone to grow old with. You will understand what I am saying later in life, by which time it may be too late," was her logic. My standard reply was, "No way". No second thought, no okay maybe I will think about it. "No way."

If she tried her, "it is important to marry and have kids in time", my favourite repartee was, "You do not need to marry to have kids," which would have her leave the room shaking her head in despair and asking the good Lord to knock some sense into me.

Marriage was not on my priority list. I had seen a couple of good medicos give up medicine after marriage because of the pressure their husband and in-laws put on them. I had no intention of going down the same road. I definitely wanted to complete my post-graduation first. In retrospect, I was also not emotionally ready.

My choice of specialisation was driven both by fascination and family. I happened to attend a spine surgery. The patient was placed prone (on his tummy) while the surgeon worked on his spine for eight hours. After the procedure, the patient was turned face up. The patient opened his eyes immediately and thanked the doctor who had put him under (the anaesthesiologist). That was fascinating, one moment the guy is on his tummy getting operated, the next he is face up thanking the doctors. All other medical specialties aim to correct the wrong; only anaesthesia first reverses normal physiology, puts people who are awake to sleep and then requires that the patient wake up after the procedure. And well, the fact that no surgical branch can work without you was also interesting. My parents also encouraged the specialty when I discussed it with them; I mean it was only a case of waiting for another three years. There were no super specialty prospects thereafter, which meant that I could not use education as an excuse to postpone marriage. I think they were secretly thrilled.

Finally at twenty-six, almost two years after my MD, after much cajoling and emotional blackmail and probably the sobering of rebellion with age, in a weak moment I consented to an arranged marriage. The logic being dad and mom would obviously ensure a good match; I mean as far as dad was concerned no boy was good enough for his daughter anyway. However, I laid down some ground rules, just three conditions really:

Condition 1: I would see no more than two boys in person and then at a venue decided by me.

Condition 2: I would entertain no photographs till the boys were shortlisted.

Condition 3: I was not to be bothered with any details till the boys were finalised.

If you are wondering why I said "two boys" it was because I made a compromise. One always needs to have a contingency plan and a choice, right? I couldn't have them select one that

I would be forced to say yes to, purely because there was no other choice...

My mother was ecstatic. She registered me on all possible marriage bureaus. The entire family: uncles, aunts, cousins, friends were all recruited for match hunting. I found my advertisement staring out at me from the matrimonial section of every English, Marathi and Punjabi newspaper under the cosmopolitan heading:

"Groom wanted for Maharashtrian doctor specialist. Slim, 5ft 5", pretty, homely, from well-to-do business family. Family of well-educated boys from respectable family, preferably non-medico, from Pune sought."

Non-medico was my requirement. I mean who wants to talk medicine at breakfast, lunch, and dinner and not to mention the possible, professional ego clashes. Pune was my mother's requirement; she wanted me to stay accessible.

I puked when I read it.

9

The first boy shortlisted was a mechanical engineer working with Kirloskar Cummins, Pune. He was a handsome, six-foot tall Punjabi boy—Randhir Sood. A heart stopper and he knew it. Against my better judgement I was coerced into visiting their house for the "seeing" programme. I had for once given in to my mom's requirements and was bedecked in a temple bordered, maroon silk saree, accompanied by a simple pearl string necklace and pearl earrings and a touch of lip-gloss. I must admit I actually looked pretty. I heard my aunt who was to accompany us heave a sigh of relief when she saw me in a sari. As for dad he seemed to be amused at the sight of me in a sari instead of my trademark jeans.

I was briefed as we drove to their bungalow in Aundh. His mother was a divorcee, a gynaecologist with a roaring practice. The boy, 'candidate number one', was a dentist with a settled practice, three years my senior, 6"2', a jetsetter who holidayed in The Alps, groomed himself in France, and wore only designer clothes. We were all welcomed very warmly. The elders settled down in the open porch while Randhir was asked to show me around the house. He was a real charmer: handsome, with sharp features, knew how to talk, had a great smile and a great sense of humour. The house was beautifully done up. As we entered his bedroom, Miss Alice, the live-in-maid, smart and only 25, followed us in. Dressed in a blue turquoise simple short shirt coupled with a flared black skirt, fair, slim, pretty, hair tied back in a loose ponytail, a hint of pink lipstick, orange blush and black eyeliner which accentuated her black eyes, she cut a pretty picture. What followed was such a cootchie-cootchie-coo scene; they spoke mostly in innuendoes and were so… intimate. That an affair was in progress was all but obvious.

Somehow, the visit ended. As we made our way home, the adults were verbose, while I kept silent. The seniors were smitten. It was a series of "Such a handsome man!" and "I think they liked you." Followed by "…and your mom-in-law is happy because she will have a doctor daughter-in-law to take over her practice". The advantages of the match were thrown back and forth in the car between mom, dad and my aunt who had accompanied us. Even our driver didn't miss a chance to say something. "Baby, sahib handsome hain."

I refused to be a party to the conversation till we got home. I went up to my room; I couldn't wait to get out of the six yards I was draped in. I cooled off before descending to the drawing room where I knew everyone was waiting. The scene was comic to say the least. My parents, the aunt who had accompanied us, and another aunt and uncle who had joined the gathering were sitting around talking in hushed tones. None of them seemed to have freshened up. They had waited for me to come and give my decision, as if none of them wanted to miss the moment. They turned in unison when they heard me enter, all of them with expectant looks on their face. I was being watched with bated breath.

All of a sudden the silence broke with each one explaining to me why I had to say yes. I refused to talk directly to anyone but my mom. I told her in no uncertain terms that Mr. Randhir Sood was Mr. Wrong. Told her that the boy would probably take after his father and go after skirts. Add to that the thought of taking over a gynaecology nursing home …ugh!

"Beta jaldi kya hain, soch lo. Aisa rishta baar baar nahin aata." (What's the hurry? Think about it. Such good matches don't come your way often.)

While we were talking, the boy's mother called to say that they were interested. It did not help matters. It only added fuel to the fire.

I stuck to my guns. The entire contingent was extremely disappointed. My aunts had already progressed to the stage of planning their wardrobes and were upset. In the next hour everybody trooped back to their homes, everyone's spirits dampened, discussing my foolishness.

Well, that was one down, one to go.

10

The second time round I was neither involved nor interested. Prima facie things seemed okay.

Ram hailed from a renowned business family who owned a chain of supermarkets. "Lucky girl, you'll get a lifetime supply of free rations. You'll never have to worry about your daily needs," was how one of my aunts' put it.

Worried that Ram was not as handsome as the first guy and I might refuse on those grounds, another advised, "You know, looks are not everything and anyways once the lights go off all guys are the same." This was Balo auntyji who had three married daughters. When they were to be wed the mantra was, "Mainu to meri kuddiya vaste tall, handsome NRI ladke hi chaide hain" (I want only tall, handsome NRI boys for my daughters)! Talk about double standards.

Mr. Ram turned out to be smart; he carried himself well and seemed OK at first dekho (sight). It was an arranged match and well there was no fault I could really find, no real reason to say no. Mr. Ram Desai M.Com., my betrothed, met and spoke to me precisely twice before the engagement. It was all non-specific, general, small talk.

I was quite neutral till the day of the engagement, which turned out to be a nightmare. The only question he asked me the whole evening while I was trying to cope with his myriad relatives was, "By the way what do you do, I mean are you a doctor, anae..." My thought was 'Anuja, run', the poor guy could not even pronounce my specialty! He wasn't even aware that I was a legitimate medical doctor. What had I let myself in for?

Two days after the engagement, he took me on a drive and we had a monologue, purely Mr. Ram in action.

"I live in a joint family. You will have to learn to adjust. Only saris, bangles and bindis and of course your mangalsutra is compulsory. No jeans, skirts not even salwar kurtas. There has been some talk about working and that you would be required to do call duties. Women from good families do not do night duties. In fact women in our family do not work. Of course, we do not want you to waste your education, you can take care of the health of the family members."

Even if I had wanted to, I couldn't have converted it into a conversation, I was (for once) lost for words. I was totally flabbergasted! How could someone talk like this in this day and age, and that too after his father had committed in an open forum that I could practice medicine. Oh and he was so... magnanimous; I was doctor enough to take care of the health of his family; be the personal physician to the Desai family, ugh!

On the half hour drive, Ram demolished six cigarettes; the guy was a chimney. By the time he dropped me off I was fuming and stinking of second hand smoke, ugh!

The next forty-eight hours were spent fretting over my situation. I was definitely not going ahead. I needed a way to do this delicately. I went for long walks. Cycled for miles. All I managed to do was exhaust myself; answers, if any, eluded me.

Normally I would have created a scene and got out. But now, I had to worry about dad and mom. Dad had just been diagnosed with high blood pressure; we were in the process of stabilizing his medicines. Plus, I mean I was an adult and had walked into the situation with my eyes open.

I tried to bring it up with my mom a couple of times. The conversation would go something like, "Ma, do you..." "Anuja, the wedding cards are so pretty. Have a look, maybe we need an extra gold line here," she would say screwing up her eyes. "What do you think?"

One time we were sitting in front of the idiot box and she was stringing beans. I was fidgety, "Mamma, I don't think..." Damn the phone. It was from the jewellers about my new wedding set.

"Yes, Lakhanji thank you so much. Yes, it will look very pretty on my Anuja." Looking in my direction. As she disconnected, I tried again, "Ma..."

"Anuja, we have to go in the morning and collect the set, it's really beautiful, you will love it," this as she collected her stuff and left the room.

Sigh, what was I to do? Looked like I was stuck with Mr. Ram. Damn! At one point I almost convinced myself that I could change the situation after marriage.

The wedding day was a month away; the countdown had already started. The venue was fixed after much deliberation by my parents. Everything had to be just right for their daughter. The wedding plans ran into three days. Sangeet, barbecue, cocktails; all the ceremonies were detailed and planned to the last T. My mom was so keen on a sangeet that she had convinced my dad to actually organise singers and a live orchestra for the evening. As for the menu... aah! The menu was agonised over for days. The final menu planned read like a dictionary from A to Z. All Indian combos from North to South, continental and Thai (all vegetarian and no alcohol, of course) cuisine were included. The house was being redecorated... I felt like a real heel for not being able to share any of the excitement. For me it was a nightmare from which I really wanted to wake up. I did everything, used every excuse in the book not to meet Mr. Ram or his family.

I found my mom giving me funny looks at times. But knowing me she just let it go probably thinking it was cold feet. The last thing she needed was for me to call the whole thing off.

Then I got a call from Ram's sister telling me that she wanted my opinion on a Honeymoon destination so that arrangements could be made. I freaked out. Reality started to kick in... Honeymoon with Mr. Ram! I got down on my knees and for once really sent up a heartfelt prayer to God to get me out of this mess. I promised to turn into a believer if he did.

11

My mom was hollering from below, "Anuja, there's a call for you."

It was 7 am on a Sunday morning, only twenty-one days to D-Day, I groaned. It was a Sunday! Decent folks should be allowed to sleep. I covered my head with a pillow.

"Anuja, she says it's urgent."

"Momma, who is it, I haven't even entered the land of the living yet."

By this time, my mom had climbed the two flights of stairs to my room and was by my bedside thrusting the cordless in my face.

"Yeah, who's this?"

"Anuja, you don't know me, but we need to meet ASAP-- please come to the South Indian Coffee Shop at 8.30 am." Then the phone went dead on me. Well, that certainly had me awake. Mysteries, I love.

I jumped out of bed, brushed, showered and dressed in a whirl of activity. My mom was surprised to see me all dressed and ready to move within half-an-hour.

"Anuja..." she said and I replied with a hug, "Will be back in a bit."

I jumped onto my "Silver Streak" as I called my Kinetic Honda and streaked off.

Parking my SS outside the coffee shop, I entered wondering how I would recognise the caller-she'd not given me her name, or a description-I shrugged. Sunday mornings at the South Indian Coffee House were chaotic. The place was packed. The aroma of filter coffee pervaded your senses as you entered.

Imagine my surprise, when I walked in to find fiancée Mr. Ram sitting on the second table to the right of the entrance. Ram had set up a surprise Sunday breakfast date? Did he have a spark, after all? Had I misjudged the guy?

That was till I saw a pretty slim girl walk up to the table balancing two cups of coffee. A sheepish Mr. Ram M.Com. stood up as I approached the table and offered me a chair.

I gave both of them my trademark look that said, "What's up?"

"Asha Bannerjee," the girl offered me her hand. She was extremely sweet, had a smiley face and was a bundle of energy; she was doing her management studies. I took in her appearance-salwar kameez, bindi, long hair tied in a neat plait, pretty.

M.Com. got us another cup of coffee as Asha filled me in. It was the usual saga-boy loved girl, girl loved boy, but an inter-caste marriage was not acceptable to their parents. Add to this the fact that Asha was a non-vegetarian and Ram's family was pure vegetarian, and you had before you a cauldron of trouble. Ram looked extremely uncomfortable during the entire exchange.

Throughout this recitation, M.Com. never said a word. I rolled my eyes, how could a lovely girl like Asha fall for a wimp like Ram. There's no accounting for taste.

"So, okay, why have you called me here? What do you want from me?"

There was a fidgety silence. Ram spoke up in a nervous voice, "Please, please refuse to marry me." Uh, oh he was shooting over my shoulder now.

"If you refuse, I can mope around for a few days and then say that I will not marry anyone except Asha."

Talk about spineless guys. I was definitely better off without him. I was miffed but hey, I had my delicate way out. I could kiss the guy if I weren't so disgusted by his spinelessness.

I wished them both all the best and ran out of the place, elated. Yippee, I sent up a grateful prayer of thanks. That was the day I was really convinced that there is someone up there who answers prayers. I was more than convinced that somebody up there was looking after me. I lost a fiancée and gained faith. Not a bad tradeoff. YIPPEEE!

I reached home. Mom was waiting at the door for me. I zoomed into the driveway on cloud nine. "Anuja, what has gotten into you? Be careful how you drive, there is hardly any time left before the wedding. Come for breakfast, the aloo parathas are waiting."

I gave her a warm hug as I sat down at the table. I heard her out while devouring my breakfast. I even took an extra paratha. Once I broke the news no one would be eating for a while. Made sense to stock up.

Then I started the process of pouring ice-cold water over my mom's well-laid out wedding plans. I took my mom into confidence and told her the whole story. She was upset initially but then came around to support my decision to pull out.

Dads can be impossible. "He'll learn to love you after marriage. The new generation and its new-fangled ideas! In India love happens after marriage."

"Give me a break dad. You conveniently forget that you had a love marriage. That your fathers were good friends and were happy with the alliance was your saving grace." I did not say it, only thought it.

Mom was my rock; she stood by me and managed to convince my dad. I could tell that dad was actually quite relieved. When the only thing he complained about was the money he lost on advances, I knew Ram had not been his idea of Mr. Right for me. Anyway, the needful was done. Thankfully, I now had the ammunition to refuse all further proposals.

Apparently, Asha and Mr. Spineless Ram Desai never did tie the knot. Lucky Asha.

So here I was at forty, a fancy-free, never married, young-at-heart cardiac anaesthesiologist, who tried her hand at whatever came her way—medical journalism, radio jockeying, wandering, exploring, reading or appreciating movies …

I was still very much connected to my parents, who worried about me incessantly, but had reluctantly resigned to my way of life.

Only now, I realised that my mom's earlier concerns had started resonating with me. Maybe I needed companionship; maybe there was a Mr. Right for me somewhere. I had actually started wondering what it would be like to have someone to grow old with.

Over the years, I had started wondering if I really loved Raghu or was just in love with the idea of loving him. But after meeting Raghu, I found myself thinking further on these lines.

Maybe my guardian angel was trying to tell me something.

12

Post the better-forgotten-reunion-of-the-famous-four, I was sleeping off the drunken revelry of the previous night. I had been restless—tossing and turning the whole night and had only managed to doze off in the wee hours of the morning. I was dead to the world. It was a Sunday morning, there was no surgery posted, I had no appointments. It was my day off. I could sleep off my hangover.

"Ring, ring, ring…" the damn cell phone.

I pulled a pillow over my head and snuggled deeper under the covers. The phone quietened down. Thank God, it felt as if chain saws were at work in my head.

"Ring, ring, ring…," Damn whoever was calling. Can't they understand that you do not wish to answer?

The ringing was driving me nuts. I reached for the mobile, cursing and writhing in agony. I tried to switch it off and landed up answering it instead, damn touch screens.

I was greeted by a cheery bright, "Good morning. I just called to thank you for bringing the group together and apologise for last night. Sorry, I left so abruptly." It was Sonali.

"Huh, I am glad you think that. I thought the evening upset you."

"It was just the suddenness of the whole thing. Anyway, after dropping you off, Raghu called and took me for a drive, we had a nice time."

Raghu, drive… a knife turned in my side.

"Anuja, we did not get a chance to catch up yesterday, why don't we meet on my return."

"Return?"

"I am in Chennai right now, attending a conference. Back by tomorrow morning."

I was feeling too miserable to mumble more than a, "Oh okay. It was great to see you. Call me once you are back, we must meet." I hung up.

My head was splitting, it was as if my eyes were on fire and there were African drums thump, thump, thumping a beat somewhere in the background. The call hadn't helped matters.

"Ring, ring, ring…," I cursed loudly, why can't people leave you alone, or at least call when you are feeling civil.

Massaging my poor head, I answered the phone and barked, "Who's this?"

"Whoa, whoa! Madam seems to have emerged from her stupor in a bad mood."

The last thing I needed was humour. "Raghu, hi, I'm in a real bad state, can we talk later?

"Talk about hanging up on friends. Charles called. He was very apologetic for yesterday. He called you but you apparently refused to answer."

Oh, so that was the called I had missed.

"Look, Charles wants to meet today around 7 pm. Guess what, he's quit drinking and wants to meet at Resham Bhavan, the tea centre at Churchgate."

"Yeah, I know the place, I'll be there. I need to get off the phone now." I hung up.

Goddamn the hangover.

I was never good at holding my drinks and normally steered clear of them. I got carried away yesterday. Feeling a wave of nausea rising, I ran to the bathroom. Made it in the nick of time. The waves of nausea just seemed to keep rising. Finally, I had nothing more to throw up, even my entrails were in the basin.

Exhausted, but definitely feeling the better for it, I downed a gallon of water, took a Disprin and forced some burnt toast and black coffee down my throat. I drew the curtains, switched off my mobile, switched on the air conditioner, and hit the sack.

The next time I surfaced it was 5 pm. The morning's conversation returned to me in snatches as I awoke; I was meeting the guys at seven. My heart warmed at the thought. I was really looking forward to meeting them. I felt much better. Good enough to have an evening out with friends.

I scrambled out of bed, I looked a mess, and I felt a mess.

13

A leisurely, tingly cold shower completed the process of waking me up. I emerged looking and feeling quite cool, if I may say so myself. I gravitate to my old ways whenever I am down. My comfort zone was blue jeans and a white T-shirt that read, 'I play to win'. Being a size twenty-eight waist after all these years was gratifying. I slipped into blue moccasins, picked up my sling, applied some light make up, a dash of lipstick, and I was out.

Resham Bhavan was a stone throw away. I lived at D Road opposite the Wankhede Stadium. I owned a two bedroom flat in Shanti Mahal. Mom had insisted on a 2BHK. "We do intend to occasionally visit." That was once in a year on my birthday for two days every year. My mom had done up the place very tastefully, organised my household, the cook, the maid, the driver, the works. The arrangements, even five years down the line, worked like a charm. Only my driver was on a month-long holiday. I hated to drive in Mumbai. Only the occasional life-or-death call from hospital would induce me to get behind the wheel. I preferred to walk or hop into a cab.

The walk with the Marine Drive cool breeze blowing in my face really felt good. Resham Bhavan is an amazing tea house. The ambience lends itself to both professional meetings and leisure outings. I reached the place on the dot at seven. Raghu and Charles were already there. Both stood up as I approached the table. I got a quick tight hug from them, followed by some compliments.

"Anuja you're really looking good."

Raghu was dressed casually: Levis and a collared, lemon yellow t-shirt, smart as usual. Charles was dressed in designer casuals. Wearing a gold Rolex on his wrist, he managed to both stand out and fit into the crowd.

"Sorry about yesterday," Charles was truly apologetic.

"No sorry" we all chorused, "...and no thanks among friends," we were all laughing now.

Charles had ordered a pot of Earl Grey for himself and Ram.

I preferred the regular masala chai.

We settled down to a hot cuppa. A comfortable silence engulfed us. It was just like old times, there had never been a need for words between us.

I reluctantly broke the silence, "The internet is a fantastic medium. If it had been around when we were in college, we would have stayed connected all this time. All these social networking sites make you feel as if you are meeting every day."

"I was amazed to hear from you after all these years. I had to read your mail twice before I could believe my eyes," said Charles.

"Anuja, your mail came at an opportune time. Your first mail arrived exactly six months to the day after I lost my wife and my life," he looked at Raghu, "I was really wondering at myself."

Both Raghu and I exchanged glances, a little uncomfortable at his sudden honesty, and muttered our condolences.

"No, no, I was feeling that way because I could not fathom my feelings. I mean I had lost my wife and I was actually happy to be a free man again. It had just started percolating in that I was free of Victoria."

"What…"

"Exactly, what I was wondering. I was happy and feeling guilty for the way I felt. Let me rewind. Raghu would probably have told you something of my troubles. Life with Victoria was a truly magical experience. We were really in love. People feel I married her only for what she had and stood for. The fact is that back then I believed both in myself and in my ability to realise my dreams. I never needed to take shortcuts… like marrying above me. Contrary to what is believed, I actually fell for Victoria the first time I saw her at the hospital charity ball. It was love at first sight. She had accompanied her father, my Chief, Dr. Cunningham."

Charles had gone dreamy. It was as if he was back at the ballroom.

"The evening was young. The charity ball was an important social do. The who's who of the medical world had made an appearance. The venue was spectacular: flowing lace curtains, glistening crystal chandeliers, ice sculptures, exotic flower arrangements, a live classical orchestra, caviar and champagne, it was the perfect setting for romance. The orchestra struck up a special tune each time a VIP entered. New to this kind of opulence, I had been craning my neck to try and identify the new arrivals.

"As the music announced another arrival my eyes turned to the door. My heart skipped a beat. The vision before me was ethereal, tall, elegant; her long, swan, neck was adorned with a single string of pearls. She wore an off-shoulder, white, fitting, designer gown. Her hair was pinned up but a few curls had broken free; left to lightly brush against her bare shoulder and her legs went on for miles. Every guy in the room was staring at her. For some reason our eyes locked across the room. Time stood still. It was just her and me. Cupid had struck, it was love at first sight.

"The Chief introduced us. We danced almost every dance together that night. Even when she was with another partner her eyes sought me out from the dance floor. She was an amazing person. Wild in some ways, innocent in others; lovable, adorable and she knew exactly how to get her way with me. She had led a very sheltered life; her every wish had been catered to. She had been wrapped in cotton wool all her life.

"The Chief encouraged the suit. He was happy to see his daughter settle down with an upcoming cardiac surgeon rather than a social stud. He kept dropping broad hints that we made a good couple and how he would be happy to have a son-in-law like me and so on.

"Victoria and me met up a couple of times after that. We talked, we laughed, we travelled, and every date was special. When I was certain that Victoria was the girl for me I went to meet the Chief to take his blessings before proposing to her. I did not want him to be surprised, and well, I had issues about whether I was good enough for her, for them. For the first time in my life my humble beginnings troubled me.

"Dr. Cunningham offered me a glass of Dom Perignon '55.

He gave me a seat and heard me out very patiently.

"He asked me only one question, 'Charles do you love her? Will you take care of my daughter?'

"I looked him in the eye and nodded."

'Welcome to the family, son. I could not have asked for a better husband for my daughter. As for the rest, I have enough of everything to take care of the next few generations; just take care of my daughter.'

"Our courtship period was fantastic. It was a fairytale story. She was undemanding; she had everything. Six months after the day I first saw her, I was walking down the aisle with her."

Both Raghu and I recalled reading the details of the entire affair in the newspapers. Even here in India it had been a big event. The press described it as the wedding of the decade. The media had followed the story very closely. It had all the ingredients, all the masala for a juicy media story-rich girl, poor boy, love at first sight.

"I was truly an orphan by then and the only family I had was Victoria and her father. Our wedding was a blur. Even today when I think of the wedding, I only see my Victoria, the Victoria I loved, floating towards me. I can almost see her now, in her white, flowing, wedding gown, a diamond tiara perched atop her petite head, smiling that and oh so radiant smile that truly lit up my life."

Charles seemed to be in a trance: eyes closed, a beautiful smile on his face. It was as though the intervening years had slipped away and he had travelled back in time.

Charles opened his eyes, and sighed."Well, the first year was an extended honeymoon; Victoria actually slipped into the wife role very comfortably. She was always there for me. Made sure I ate on time, gave me space when I needed it, cut down on her partying and although she enjoyed her alcohol every now and then, she actually became a purely social drinker. It was picture perfect. We took off on weekends, spent quality time together, had fun.

"We had the first inkling of trouble in paradise after Alex II was born. Victoria slipped into postpartum depression. We did not realise it at first. I had gone back to a full operating schedule. Victoria became an alcoholic before anyone of us realised. The Chief was extremely supportive through it all. He spent a lot of time with Alex II and in fact Alex used to be more with him than us. The kid stayed on track and developed his set of values from his grandfather. Victoria was in and out of rehab.

"Dr. Cunningham died when Alex II was fourteen. He had returned home after watching Alex II lift the school league trophy as Captain of his football team. Having spent the evening celebrating with Alex, he had driven back late at night. He called me complaining of chest pain at two the next morning. The emergency medical team was alerted as I rushed to his side. I found him in the drawing room on the sofa, without a pulse. He was rushed to hospital. He had suffered a massive heart attack and was declared dead on arrival.

"His death was literally the nail in the coffin of our marriage. Thereafter there was no reasoning with Victoria. Things just fell apart. Victoria and I were fighting all the time. For some unknown reason Victoria blamed me for the death of the Chief. She felt I did not do anything to save him even though I was by his side. Our equations changed in many ways. The sudden, unexpected death of the Chief left Victoria in control of everything. Everything was in her name. Our pre-nuptial contract (which the Chief had insisted on to protect Victoria) had been made in such a way that if I left her, I would walk away from everything I had worked for.

"I had started enjoying the attention, the favours, the pleasures and the luxuries that money can buy. It's amazing how one slips into such a way of life so easily. Somewhere along the way I had started thinking of it as compensation for the hell Victoria was putting me through. I stayed on in a lifeless and loveless marriage. Victoria took to taunting me in public. I had seriously begun to contemplate leaving her. To hell with everything! Things came to such a head that we couldn't be in the same room without breaking things. This bitter environment drove Alex II further away from us.

"Victoria became a shrew. Life became miserable at home. The only saving grace was my work. By then I had established myself as a name in Cardiac Surgery and had made my own niche. I was more than just Victoria's husband or the Cunningham son-in-law. I started spending more time in hospital. There were days on which I would check myself into a hotel just to get a good night's sleep. "

Charles nervously ran a hand through his hair, as he continued, "I remember the night she died. It had been a long haul at work; back-to-back surgeries. I had scrubbed out and found innumerable missed calls from Victoria and messages that were mostly abusive. Right then I had thought of checking into a hotel for another night."

Running his hand through his hair he said, "I sat in my office for a while. Initially I thought of calling. Then I realised it would end in the usual way; a slanging match or worse. For some reason that I cannot still fathom even to date, I decided that I needed to go home that night. It was the Christmas weekend. It was quite late when I reached. The house was all lit up. The Christmas tree was standing in our living room and had been decorated. It was a Friday night. The house help had the evening off. I let myself in. I looked up as I entered to see Victoria standing at the top of the staircase. She probably heard me enter; it was as though she had stayed up waiting for me to arrive.

Dressed in a flowing black negligee, a full glass of wine in her hand. She was slightly unsteady and held the railing to steady herself. The moment she saw me, something broke inside her; she went berserk. She started screaming at me, accusing me for spoiling her life and killing her father. She threw her glass at me. I stepped aside as it hit the wall beside me and splintered into a million little fragments. The next thing I knew she was rushing down the stairs towards me, mad with rage. And then, as if in slow motion, I saw her lose her balance as she tripped on her negligee and literally rolled down the stairs. The last image I have of her is of her small body laid out on the marble floor at the bottom of the staircase, her neck bent at an unnatural angle, a pool of blood forming around her head like a fiery, red halo. The colour drained from her face. She was as white as the marble floor; lifeless...yet angelic even in death...

"My son Alex, walked in as I was crouched over her, cradling her in my arms. His eyes were full of hurt and sadness, 'You killed her' he said, with tears rolling down his cheeks, 'Don't bother looking for me'. It was the last thing he said to me as he ran out of the front door. He did not wait to hear anything. Did not stop... I had to call in the medics. I couldn't go after him."

Charles' eyes were wet. He blinked rapidly to hide his tears. "He came for her funeral. I saw him watching from a distance. Never said a word to anyone. Avoided meeting me. The place was thronging with people wanting to offer their condolences. I kept pushing them out of the way to reach him, but by the time I got to where I had seen him, he had disappeared again. I really wonder how he has coped all these years," sighed Charles.

"I was a suspect, considering the fortune I came into. Many people thought I had killed Victoria for her fortune. Our personal life was made an open book. Over the next few months there was a lot of questioning, a lot of people were left unconvinced by my explanation. The homicide department of the police were called in, a coroner was called. Our house was cordoned off; it was being regarded as a crime scene. I was the chief murder suspect. I made the news for all the wrong reasons. Every news channel you turned on had my face plastered all over it. The talk shows were adjudicating my innocence with each side going into lengthy monologues on what they assumed to be my character traits, as though they were my closest of friends. They finally had to let me go for lack of evidence. The autopsy confirmed accidental death. To be honest, I do sometimes wonder if I was responsible for her death in a way. If I had stayed in a hotel that night instead of going home or reached home earlier, before she became really drunk. If only things had worked out differently, I actually miss her..."

If only... Were we all plagued by it?

"It's real sad when you can't even mourn in private. It's even sadder when the one person who is family is not with you in such a time of sorrow. I wanted to be there for my son at least then. I had failed him yet again.

"I waited. I thought he would come home once the anger settled. After a couple of months I realised it would not happen. I then started activating my contacts to help trace my son. He seemed to have just disappeared from the face of the earth. Having contacts in high places helps. The Indian High Commissioner called me last week to say that Alex was in India. He apparently came in two months ago. I am here to search for him. He always wanted me to bring him to India and show him the country. Stories of the palaces, the maharajahs, rope tricks, elephant rides have always fascinated him, just as it does all foreigners. Guess he decided to explore it on his own."

He sighed.

Raghu and I looked at each other. I felt for Charles. Everything yet nothing. "But come, that's a lot of water under the bridge. I feel better after offloading my woes on to you guys. I plan to find Alex and start afresh. I am looking forward to a new beginning. Now that I know where to start looking for Alex I am feeling better. Fill me in with what you have been up to."

Our chicken sandwiches and stir-fried prawns had arrived. The mood around the table lightened as we dug into our food, laughing while recalling our days in college, and sharing stories of those parts of our lives that we had missed out on.

It was 9:30 pm, and I needed my eight-hour beauty sleep to be ready for the next week.

I reluctantly pushed back my chair, picked up my sling and pecked the guys on their cheeks (that's the liberty one can take with old friends), got a peck from each guy in return (Yippee! From Raghu as well). I was chivalrously escorted to the door after having refused their offers to drop me home. Leaving the men together, I left.

I needed my fresh air. I had a lot to think about. "You have a message..." my mobile chirped.

"Hi! Sorry I caught you at the wrong time in the morning. Looking forward to catching up. Take care, good night – Sonali." It read I smiled. Friends. It was good to have them back in my life. I floated home on a cloud.

I reached home and drifted into a dreamless sleep.

Probably if I had known that I would be 'the' topic of conversation with the guys for the next half an hour I would have turned myself into the proverbial fly on the wall.

It appears that I don't need clocks or alarms of any kind in the morning. It's as though wake up calls get automatically scheduled on my phone. Without fail, every single day, the ringing of my mobile jolts me out of slumber. "Ring, ring…"

"Hello," I said sleepily rubbing my eyes. For God sake, it was already 8.30 am! I had overslept; I jumped out of bed while talking. Phone tucked between my shoulder and left ear I continued talking while making up the bed.

"Good morning, ma'am, this is Dr. Sekhar from Forum Hospitals. The Director wanted to meet sometime this week at your convenience. When can we schedule the meeting?"

I mentally accessed my weekly schedule. The week was packed.

"The earliest I can commit to is next Saturday," I said, my mobile tucked between my left ear and shoulder. I folded the sheets and plumped the pillows.

"Yes ma'am. I will confirm and call back. Thank you."

That gave me six days to take a decision, to accept or not accept. The money was good, but I would be shifting from a very relaxed routine to a regimented, rota system. But now there was the Raghu angle which had to be considered.

I shook myself. There was enough time to think things through. "Get on with it girl or you'll be real late!" I showered quickly, gulped down my cornflakes and rushed to work.

My first case was that of Mr. Patel who was scheduled for a cardiac bypass surgery. The operating surgeon, Dr. Thomas, had musical hands. He played the heart like a symphony during the beating heart surgery . In and out in three hours; three total arterial grafts, stable pressures; smooth. My surgeons spoilt me. Leaving the chest closure to his assistant, Dr. Thomas scrubbed out. After being used to such excellent surgical hands and results, I shuddered at the stories from other cardiac anaesthesiologists of beating hearts taking eight and ten hours and with poorer success rates. The patient shifted and settled in to his recovery room. Now we were in for a long wait—the patient scheduled next was trying to mobilise resources.

After an hour of waiting, the second case was cancelled at the last minute. The reason—lack of availability of blood and the patient's inability to pay the all-important deposit. Vitamin M (Money) deficiency plagues everything including the operative list.

Quite unexpectedly I found myself at a loose end. It gave me an opportunity to catch up with Sonali.

"Hi Sonali," I said a bit hesitantly because she had answered on the very first ring, "How are you placed today? Could we meet for coffee or dinner?"

Sonali was very enthusiastic, "The earlier the better. Let's make it an early dinner."

I decided to finish my pre-anaesthetic check-ups before heading home. I asked the Operating Theatre staff to check the operation list for the next day. We had two cases posted-a lung surgery and a cardiac bypass.

We were to start with Professor Khanna, a Bombay University Professor of Economics, who had been admitted for a cardiac bypass surgery. The second case was Mrs. Menon, a forty-five-year-old suffering from lung cancer admitted for removal part of her lung; I had already reviewed her case.

"Ma'am, Professor Khanna is in the cardiac recovery room (the immediate pre operative and post operative cardiac rooms) nine."

Thanking sister, I went to visit Professor Khanna while still in my scrubs. The gentleman was an active fifty-five-year-old; healthy, with no co-morbid conditions like hypertension and diabetes. He was a non-smoker and did not have a family history of heart disease. Professor Khanna had been diagnosed with 100 per cent blockages of all the three main arteries of the heart and had shown abnormal heart rhythms in his cardiac work-up. He was sitting up comfortably hooked to the monitor (which showed a regular heart rate of 88 per minute and a non-invasive blood pressure of 130/80 mm Hg) reading a newspaper when I entered.

I greeted him with a smile, shook his hand and introduced myself. In a bid to make him comfortable I said, "Professor Khanna, you do not look like a patient at all. Are you sure you are in the right place?"

That did it. Professor Khanna turned violent,"That is what I am telling all the doctors. I strongly suspect that this is some kind of racket. I am perfectly fine. Every day I climb five floors up to my department in college without any symptoms, I walk seven kilometres a day, I gym, I have no bad habits, no family history. I go in for regular medical check-ups and you diagnose me with heart blocks that are so severe that I have to be operated at a day's notice. This is a moneymaking racket. I do not need surgery."

By now Professor Khanna was yelling, and had turned red in the face, the monitor was going crazy; the most erratic and dangerous ventricular tachyarrhythmia was playing out on the screen.

While he was talking I had examined and noted what I needed to. With a "Professor Khanna, the cardiologists and surgeons are only doing the best for you, take care and see you tomorrow," I literally ran from the cubicle. The last thing I needed was for him to arrest on me. Given the blocks in his heart vessels it was unlikely we would have been able to revive him.

I changed out of my scrubs and made a couple of social visits to some of my patients before heading home.

15

Come evening and I was dressed in jeans and a flaming red t-shirt walking Sonali to Kamling for some scrumptious Chinese food. The ambience was just what we needed: happy and quiet. Being a weeknight, we pretty much had the place to ourselves.

We were escorted to a table for two. Thanking the captain we took our seats. Sonali was looking radiant, she hadn't aged a day, and the only fault I could find was that her smile did not quite reach her eyes. Even dressed in blue jeans; a blue, round-necked t-shirt; and wearing just a hint of lip-gloss, she made heads turn. Her penchant for oversized bags did not seem to have changed. Guess the more we age, the same we stay.

The Captain took our order for, "Whatever you recommend". Both of us refused alcoholic drinks and settled for some fresh lime soda instead.

"So tell me, where have you been, what have you been up to?" "Anuja, you are the only one I could really talk to, bare my soul to. You have always kept my secrets."

"I am done with running. I have finally realised that you cannot run from yourself. Places change, people change, situations change, you don't."

Déjà vu. All my friends seem to have rehearsed their lines together. Everyone seems to have come full circle.

"I could see you recalling the circumstances in which we last met at dinner."

"First I want to thank you for just being there that day. It made the whole sordid affair just about bearable."

Our soup arrived. I stopped her in her tracks, although I was itching to know the details.

"Sonali, let's just enjoy the food and each other's company for now; talk about the pleasant things in life. We'll keep the serious stuff for later."

With the ice broken, Sonali transformed before my eyes, she visually relaxed. As we started talking the glow, the animation all reappeared. What ensued was a hilarious, fun-filled evening. It was as if the intervening years never happened. We discussed books, movies, music everything except our personal lives. We talked about professors and all the classic moments of college life that gave rise to unforgettable phrases such as "Open the doors of the window", "Put your platelets (plaits) into your apron", and finally, "Divide yourself into four trays". Our anatomy class had a lecturer who certainly had an axe to grind with the English language.

Sonali seemed to have been in touch with some of our other college mates.

"Remember Ali, the software geek who almost dropped out of medical college because he had floated his own software company and was getting lot of work. I mean he was talking lacs when we were talking hundreds."

"Yeah, in fact it was Charles and Raghu who had prevailed on him to finish his final year. What about him?"

"He finished his medicine as well as a Diploma in Pediatrics while running his software company, which continued to prosper. He started running his aunt's pediatric practice near Swarg Gate. Well, apparently a couple of years down the line the municipal corporation took away half the clinic premises as part of a road widening programme. Taking it as a sign of divine intervention that he should not practice medicine anymore, he turned to professional photography and is now an official photographer with the National Geographic. He married a software girl who looks after the software company while he travels the world!"

Talk about a quirk of fate! Some guys appear to have their cake and eat it too.

Dinner was done by around nine thirty. Feeling really relaxed we walked out of Kamling. Impulsively, Sonali grabbed my arm and said, "Anuja, let's go to my hotel room and continue from where we left off earlier." It was then revealed to me that she was staying at the Oberoi itself. I am so bad at garnering the details of a person's living arrangements. "Where are you staying, who are you staying with, how are you commuting, why are you in Mumbai," were questions that suddenly started suggesting themselves to me. It left me wondering where Charles and Raghu were putting up. Curious and keen to learn the details I let her lead on.

She was on the seventh floor, in a sea-facing room. You couldn't ask for a more perfect room. It was aesthetically done up and gave an impression that you were actually sitting by the seashore. The moment we entered Sonali kicked off her stilettos.

She settled down on the sofa with her feet tucked under her, and patted the seat near here, "Make yourself comfortable."

Slipping out of my moccasins, I also curled up hugging a cushion.

Sonali played the perfect hostess. She fetched water for the two of us and then said, "Can I order something?"

"Some coffee should be perfect."

"No coffee for you at night. You never could sleep after a caffeine fix." She remembered how coffee always got me highly strung! Sonali ordered hot chocolate for both of us.

Sonali had a resigned look on her face as she settled back to tell her story. "Anuja, let me start from my shift to Delhi. After medical school as you know I moved to Delhi. What you don't know is that I really moved there because of Shubham."

"Dr. Shubham Mehra...?"

"Don't look so shocked. You already know he was the college Casanova. He really knew the art of persuasion. He pursued and wooed me. By the time I finished medical school I was really smitten.

"He got his residency at Sir ASL Gana Hospital, Delhi. It was a purely surgical setup. I took up gynaecology at St Mary's. At least we would be in the same city. Shubham arranged the residency for me.

"The first six months after landing in Delhi, we painted the town red. We were adjusting our duties, working around our shifts and making time to meet. We were studying, working, courting; it was an amazing time. Within six months, Shubham was offered a fortuitous senior residency position and was really excited.

"The troubles started thereafter. His workload increased. Both our residencies became heavy, both being surgical specialties, getting time off became difficult. We seemed to be at cross-purposes. Time together dwindled. I left messages that never got answered. Every time I tried to get in touch, it was a case of "Dr. Shubham is busy he'll call back. Even when he came on the phone he was casual, he always had an excuse for not being able to meet. At times, he even got irritated and suggested that I was getting 'clingy'. Initially I took these signs at face value even though it hurt... till almost four months later."

She sighed as she took a sip of water, twirling the water in the glass, the memories were definitely not happy. After a minute of complete silence, she seemed to shake herself into the present, "Sorry. Well, Dr. Rajan a surgical registrar joined our hospital for an allied posting. I would bump into him quite often at the cafeteria, the corridor, the wards, or operating theatres. At times I thought he wanted to say something but hesitated. From my experience with guys I generally preferred it that way, what they came up with could at times spoil relationships. Anyway, one day I was sitting alone in the cafeteria having coffee, lost in thought when Rajan approached me like a man on a mission."

'Dr. Sonali, I have been told that you are very close to Dr. Shubham.'

"I was pissed. I mean it was none of his business. I got up in a huff ready to leave, wondering about who had been kind enough to give him the details of my personal life. With the way things were between Shubham and me, I had become ultra-sensitive.

'Dr. Sonali, please sit down. I have come to respect you and do not like to see you, well, down because of someone like Shubham.'

"Now, he had my attention. What did he mean by someone like Shubham? I sat down, and it was a good thing I did. The next couple of minutes, my world started to spin out of control."

'Shubham is having an affair with his colleague and co-resident Reshma. In fact they have been living in for the last three months.' The words came out in a rush.

Sonali had a wry smile as she continued, "I was stunned. I did not know how to react. I hated Rajan for what he was telling me. I could have killed Shubham barehanded. He was romancing his co-resident while keeping me hanging and actually had the audacity to call me clingy!

"I did not know whether to cry or be mad. I kept my head, thanked Dr. Rajan for the information, shook hands with him and very coolly walked away. The poor guy did not know what to do, he was left sitting at the table with a troubled expression on his face. He probably expected me to throw myself into his arms and cry on his shoulder.

"As a matter of fact, I was shattered. My legs were unsteady. I was really hurt and angry. Yet, I needed to hear it from Shubham himself. Call it what you want: childish, immature, whatever, but I needed to know from him if what Rajan had said was true. He continued to refuse to take my calls, refused to meet or talk to me. It was as if we had never existed as a couple. My social life had been mothballed since my shift to Delhi so I had no one to turn to. My life had centred on Shubham so life started to lose meaning. I was starting to lose my grip and I had gone into a shell; food and sleep meant nothing anymore and the days and weeks seemed to merge together. That was about the time that Charles joined my institution."

"You had written to me about it."

Our hot chocolate arrived; an unnecessary interruption, I was really engrossed in her story. Sending off room service at the earliest, we settled down with our chocolate, "So, what happened?" I said.

"Charles became my support system. He was a real sweetheart. He did not ask questions, did not push me in any way. Initially we picked up where we had left off in college. He would wait for me; take me for drives. He had acquired an old 1967 Fiat. We went for midnight drives to India Gate, late night movies, coffee and kebabs. He slowly drew me out and although hurt I definitely felt much better. Once I began to talk about what had happened and how hurt I was, my own mental state changed. I actually started to enjoy life again, although somewhere a hollowness persisted."

She took a pause, as if in deep thought and then seemed to shake herself, "Imagine my surprise when three months down the line Charles told me that he had always been infatuated with me and wanted to be more than friends. However, he promised not to push me, since he did not want me making any hasty decisions in the state I was in.

"I was going through a bad time and was only too happy to have a known shoulder to cry on. After knowing the way he felt about me I felt grateful for his understanding and support. He was a darling and really looked after me. After, almost a year of dating, he started proposing to me. I was not quite ready but found myself actually thinking about it."

"Charles?" I was stumped, or was I? Every guy in college had probably harboured "feelings" for Sonali. But then, why was Charles so rude to Sonali now? Questions, questions... that I would ask later. I did not want to break the flow.

"Then the unimaginable happened. Shubham started pursuing me again. Out of the blue, he started calling me up. I initially refused to take his calls. Then he started working on my friends. To date I do not know what caused the change of heart. Cards, red roses, phone calls, hand delivered letters. I resisted initially; he had really hurt me."

Lucky girl. Two guys. All the works. Sigh. Where was all this leading? I was really impatient to hear the rest now.

"Ring, ring…," damn my cell.

I looked at the number. It was our resident, Dr. Akhtar Hussain, Zaks, calling. I gave Sonali an apologetic look and answered it.

"Good evening Ma'am. We need to re-explore the morning coronary bypass case, Mr. Patel. He's drained a litre. He drained 300 ml in the first three hours but then it was 25 to 50 every hour. In the last two hours he's suddenly drained 500, the drains are full. Suspect it is from the sternal wires. Patient vitals are stable."

"Arrange the blood and blood products, keep the OT ready and call in the on-call anaesthesiology resident. I will be there in ten minutes."

Sonali was already on her feet, collecting my stuff. I gave her a quick apologetic hug and promising to call, I rushed to the hospital.

16

The OT was ready when I reached. Fortunately for us, Mr. Patel's breathing tube had not been removed and he was still on the ventilator. This made things simpler for us. We wheeled him into the OT. The surgical residents had the patient painted and draped before the on-call cardiac surgeon, Dr. Akash, scrubbed in. Dr. Thomas had left for Delhi soon after the surgery.

Dr. Akash was of middle height with a "well-developed" midriff, all the better to hold the patients on the table with. He was grumpy, upset at the resident who had closed the chest the first time. Akash had the poor night staff scurrying around, they couldn't seem to do anything right. The instruments were bad, the suction kept getting blocked and blood products though available, were taking time to reach the theatre. All in all, the going was anything but smooth. The re-exploration went on till the wee hours. As happens a lot of the time, there was no obvious bleeder, a good saline wash and closure was all that was required. His chest closed, our patient settled back into recovery, I made my way home. A grumpy surgeon and unnecessary screaming sessions are not conducive to a good night's sleep.

I was restless. Sonali was on my mind. I tried everything— hot milk, a hot shower. I couldn't seem to fall asleep. No mangalsutra, no wedding band. Two guys, one had been married, Manju, what had happened...? I drifted off trying to figure out the jigsaw. All in all it was a bad night.

A bad night before equals a bad day for me. I was in a sour mood the next morning. I needed to hear the complete story. It was not as if I could just pick up the phone and ask Sonali...

Work kept me occupied, mentally busy and on my feet. Sonali was pushed to the back of my mind, but I harboured this niggling feeling that I needed to call her soon to know the rest of her story.

On Wednesday, my surgeon had to leave town urgently and all procedures were rescheduled. It's crazy how we anaesthesiologists cannot plan our lives. The surgeon needs to take-off so surgery gets cancelled; if an anaesthesiologist needs time off... there's the devil to pay.

"But wait", I thought, it would give me the time I needed to catch up with Sonali. I called her and planned a ladies day out-lunch and shopping. Yes, something to look forward to.

I picked Sonali up in a cool cab from The Oberoi and we made our way to Phoenix Mills.

It was as if we were back in college. We visited all the sales, all the branded shops, tried everything, and bought nothing. We had a ball. We took a "candy floss" break and laughed when the gooey stuff stuck to our faces. Thank God I did not bump into any of my patients or colleagues.

We decided to try our hand at the bowling alley. In the first round, my finger got stuck in the ball and I found myself halfway down the alley before Sonali rescued me. I had these ten-year olds waiting in line, who rolled their eyes and gave me a look that seemed to say, "Man, you don't even know how to bowl".

Lunch was at Mac Donald's. We decided on the happy meal. The cuddle toys they were giving out were real cute. Extremely happy and content, licking double-scoop, chocó-chip ice cream in waffle cones, we made our way back to South Mumbai.

By mutual consent, we stopped the cab at Chowpatty. The evening was cool, the sea was quiet and shimmered with an alluring shade of blue. We slipped out of our shoes and folded our trousers. Shoes dangling in one hand we walked along the water line, the small waves just breaking at our feet and gently spraying us with salty sea water. The sand felt cool and good.

Spotting a good spot to park our backsides, we decided to sit down and experience the sunset. We made ourselves comfortable, our chins rested on our arms which were folded around our knees.

Trickling sand through my fingers, I couldn't contain my curiosity anymore. I broached the subject that had been troubling me. In fact, I blurted it out, "Sonali, whom did you marry? Shubham or Charles?"

Sonali laughed loudly, "I was wondering when you would broach the subject. I knew not hearing my complete story must be bothering you. I am surprised you waited so long to ask."

She got a look from me that said, "Please, please break the suspense".

17

"It was Shubham," Sonali said, going into a trance.

"I was confused so I decided to take a three-month break from work. I moved to my aunt's place, Saroj auntyji, who had just undergone a knee replacement and was happy for my company. Shubham pursued me. He was relentless with his calls and messages. I tried to ignore him. He worked on my aunt and had her eating out of his hand. 'Puttar (child),' she said '... he's a very nice guy. You are lucky he cares so much for you. Forgive him. The fact that he has come back means he really cares about you. I guess distance does make the heart grow fonder.'

"Apparently, Dr. Reshma had been in love with him and had managed to seduce him in a moment of weakness. He had then avoided me not knowing how to handle the situation. But, over the months he realized that I was the one for him. Hence the new efforts.

" I guess, I should have known better. In retrospect, I do not know whether I was really so blind in love or it just gave my ego a boost to know that I was not rejected. Anyway, he worked his charm on me again.

"Shubham organised a perfect candlelight dinner for me on my birthday. A romantic serenade was playing in the background, the room was decorated with orchids. He had placed an engagement ring at the bottom of my champagne glass and then before I realised it he got down on one knee. It was perfect, I was so overcome with emotions, I accepted. We kissed right there oblivious to all those around.

"Fortunately, since he was a Punjabi, my parents did not have any issues.

He was handsome, a doctor, from a good, solid Punjabi background.

"Like my aunt said, 'Thank God, love bhi kiya to Punjabi se'.

"Shubham's father was a darling; he accepted me, at least on those occasions when we were sharing a one-to-one conversation. His mother was a different story. She was extremely upset. She looked daggers at me all the time and never failed to take digs at me whenever we were alone together. She had expected to get a better 'deal' for her son. She went on and on like a broken record about the 'good offers' she had received for her son. Oh and she was very careful to do it while Shubham was out of hearing range. The rest of the time she behaved sickly sweet; even sugar wouldn't melt in her mouth. In short, she was the typical mom- in-law.

"Shubham has an elder brother, Rakesh. He had shifted to the US two years before our marriage. A software engineer, he had made his parents take a loan to finance him. His parents were all gaga about their 'Amerikewala beta (son in America)'. Rakesh's successful immigration had them dreaming about travelling to America. They hoped he would send them air tickets and eventually help them become American citizens once he got his green card and settled down there.

"In the initial days Rakesh called regularly. He made sure his financial needs were catered to. After all 'America is expensive'. Once he settled down and got a job, the frequency of his calls started dwindling. In fact after his marriage to an American girl just three months later they had stopped altogether. He had spoken to Shubham and as good as hinted that he was unlikely to return and definitely would not be taking any responsibility for his parents. Initially Shubham kept his own counsel. But the constant Amerikewala beta dialogues took their toll on him and he had to ensure that the parents understood that Rakesh was neither coming back nor interested in their welfare. His father had realised and accepted the news calmly. His mother on the other hand stopped praising her Amerikewala beta in the privacy of the home, but continued with her 'mera Amerikewala beta' dialogues in public. But thereafter, she became extremely possessive about Shubham.

"Newly engaged, I was on cloud nine and refused to let her dampen my spirits. I actually felt sorry for her, considering that she'd had all her hopes pinned on the elder son. She had also had all the possible rich'matches' lined up for him and the whole thing had just backfired. Having a son in America is like owning Fort Knox. And of course socially speaking the possibility of going to America was a major prestige issue for her. After all, almost all the families related to her had at least one child settled abroad and all their parents were 'America return'. Only now when she talked of America her attention was actually on Shubham whom she now relied upon for the realisation of all her other dreams."

"Anyway we were to stay on in Delhi and his parents lived at Jalandhar. I could handle her cold waves long distance. Shubham was my rock; he insisted on my rejoining St Mary's and taking my MD exams."

I interrupted, "What happened to Charles?"

She brushed the question aside, "He had left to pursue his cardiac surgery dream and moved to the US by the time I rejoined.

"Anyway, I got back to my work routine. Both Shubham and I finished our respective specialisations. That year was the best ever. We were so much in love and Shubham seemed to have finally decided to mend his wandering ways. It was a dream wedding. With Shubham everything had to be glamorous and just right.

"He planned the whole wedding to the last detail, our clothes, the sangeet with choreographed dances and the food. In short, it's a wedding people still discuss. It was the typical 'Big Fat Punjabi wedding' that you see in movies.

"We moved into a plush two-bedroom-hall-kitchen apartment in Delhi, bought a car and were very comfortable and, most importantly, very much in love. Shubham took the plunge into private practice.

"Our career graphs were progressing well. We worked hard, we played hard."

Sonali trickled sand through her fingers, stared into the waters as she continued, transported back in time, "Our idyllic state of marriage lasted all of six months. Shubham's father suffered a stroke and was paralysed along his left side. His parents moved in with us. After all they had only us and both of us being doctors ensured that he received proper medical care. Shubham really looked after him in every way but unfortunately, we lost him in a couple of weeks. Even during this time, mataji showed no signs of mending her ways. She was constantly on my case.

"After Shubham's father passed away, mataji decided to move in permanently.

Thereafter I could do nothing right. The whole day she would be lording it in the house and when Shubham was expected to return she would be in the kitchen getting tea ready and fussing over what Shubham liked, as if she had been at it the whole day. And Shubham was like 'Let her be. You have your work. Let her take care of the house; it will keep her busy.' Men can be so insensitive.

"Mataji refused to go out. Even on the occasions when Shubham convinced her that she needed to go out she would develop mysterious headaches once both of us were ready and had one foot out of the door. We couldn't leave mataji alone at home of course. So we would all stay home and I would find myself cooking dinner at the last minute. It really bugged me. Taking advantage of the fact that I kept erratic working hours, everything in the house was played around with. I would come back to find the furniture rearranged to her convenience, stuff in the drawing room moved around, cupboards rearranged, stuff that I had put away was discarded. In everything mataji knew best and orders had to be followed. God forbid if you protested, she never missed a chance to play martyr.

"She was the queen of melodrama. Her entire attitude towards us hinged on the belief that 'now that I am old and alone, you can say what you want to me and I have to listen'. Also, 'this would never have happened if my husband were alive'.

"God bless his soul, he was probably better off dead than living with the shrew."

Sonali really sounded disillusioned. In all the time I had known her she had always been a generous, giving, and understanding person. These were real harsh words coming from her.

Sonali caught me staring at her.

"She had never really forgiven me for marrying her son. A bigger better bakra (sacrificial goat) is what she had planned. And now with her husband gone, she was really insecure as well as in the right position to derive maximum emotional mileage from her situation. She made every effort to make things intolerable. She wanted to hog the little time that Shubham spent at home.

"My maids walked out, no one lasted for more than a week; the record was an hour. Even then I was willing to accept everything. I truly wanted her to be comfortable with us. After all Shubham was all the only family she had. I kept hoping her better senses would prevail at some point of time."

"Still… there were times when I became very upset and frustrated. I could not understand why we had to shoulder the brunt of taking care of her when her elder son was living such a cushy life. He made no personal or financial commitment of any kind. In fact, after his father's death, he hadn't even come down to visit. It was the usual excuse: 'No leave. I have a visa problem. There were no tickets available'. And then once all the last rites were over it did not make sense for him to come down. Although he had made phone calls during the two weeks of his father's illness about how worried and concerned he was, when it actually mattered he couldn't come. He started calling up his mother almost every day. Initially Shubham and I were happy for her, till we realised that he was only playing her. Shubham's dad had literally cut him out of his life. Now, with him gone he started telling my mom-in-law how he was going through a financial crisis and needed finances to start up a business. He started promising to take her with him again. Slowly but surely, he staked his claim to the property. And my mom-in-law was like, 'My Amerikewala puttar! We must help him.' So the ancestral house was sold. After all, in her words, 'tum log to waha aaoge nahi, aur mein to akele nahi reh sakti' (you guys are never going to move there and I cannot stay alone). The proceeds were promptly transferred to the US of A. Thereafter of course the calls became more infrequent. He called once a week, then once a fortnight and then his calls were fewer and further apart.

"Now, it was more than certain that she was not going anywhere. I dug my heels in and started seriously trying to make life bearable in the house. In spite of all my efforts things got worse. She started her 'convert Shubham' campaign. She started taunting me for not conceiving. 'You people are not getting younger, it's already a year. Just because you are a gynaecologist you think you know everything.'

"Every visitor who came was told about the fact that we had a 'five year family plan'.

"She did not realise that she was actually hitting where it hurt most. Shubham and I were not practicing any form of contraception and we were an active couple. I was also worried.

"I spoke to Shubham and found out that he was not in any hurry to become a father. He kept telling me that he was happy to be just a husband for now. After much persuasion he agreed to go along with my suggestion of visiting the experts. Then started the rounds of tests and investigations. Shubham had a low sperm count. The stud in him was very hurt. It took much persuasion but Shubham agreed to begin IVF (In Vitro

Fertilisation) treatment. The process was long and testing: my fertility cycle, the hormonal injections, ova harvesting. His mother was not told anything so she continued nagging us. She started becoming a big pain.

"The stress of the decision, mental strain, and the rigorous nature of the treatment procedures were probably responsible for nullifying all our efforts. Cycle after cycle failed. Shubham started withdrawing from the whole thing.

"I guess everything started getting to him. He started drinking heavily, became erratic, his practice suffered. I on the contrary took solace in my work. My practice flourished; probably my own failure to conceive actually made me happy to be a part of the process for others. I had started earning more than Shubham. In an ironical twist, all that was happening at home pushed me to do better at the work place.

"Even that worked against us. Everyone that Shubham met insisted on telling him what a successful wife he had and how he no longer needed to work; he could actually retire, they said. Shubham hit the bottle harder. He became abusive and violent after his drinking sprees. During the lull periods there was silence, an accusatory silence. Bruises and cut lips became commonplace."

Sonali a victim of domestic violence! Seemed surreal.

"I kept hoping that things would improve. They didn't, they got worse. With work dwindling, he started spending more time at home with his mom. She started poisoning him against me, telling him what a mistake he had made. How he could still do better for himself. He started spending all his time in front of the idiot box watching all the serials with her. His drinking increased, he developed tremors, his non-existent practice folded up. Life became hell. The house was full of empty liquor bottles wherever you looked.

"His mother took over our lives. She blamed me for everything that had gone wrong with her son. She would curse me and now Shubham stopped trying to shield me from her. If he found it uncomfortable he would just leave the room. It was the only exercise he was getting at that time."

Sonali was really bitter. She continued, biting her lower lip to stop it from trembling, "One fine day, I came home to find my stuff packed and in the hall. There was no protest from Shubham. Mataji knew best. I moved out."

Sonali recalled with a frown, "When I found my bags packed and at the door I was devastated. I expected my husband to do more. But, as statistics clearly state, educated successful women carry the highest rate of marital torture. Something broke inside me. Without a word I picked up my bags. Tears streaming down my face I walked to the lift. I almost fell over my bags, my vision blurred by a film of tears. I somehow called myself a cab and checked into Hotel Imperial opposite the hospital."

"I was in Delhi. A single tear-stained woman checking in alone into a hotel at eleven in the night raised quite a few eyebrows. I locked myself into my room and placed a Do Not Disturb board outside. I switched my mobile and TV off for four days. It was like I was creating my own cocoon.

"The tears flowed till none were left. I had more angry conversations with the good Lord than I have had during my entire life. I slept fitfully, did not know whether it was day or night. The housekeeping guys were worried and every once in a while they called on the pretext of checking out if I needed something. They probably thought that I was a potential candidate for suicide. I suppose discovering the body of a guest in their hotel room is not good for business.

"Anyway, I guess I was stronger than I realised or too chicken to commit suicide, I still don't know which. On the fifth day I decided that enough-was-enough. 'Welcome to the real world Sonali' I thought bitterly.

"I picked myself up, shopped till I dropped, treated all my senses to the best experiences in the market—Ayurvedic massages, five star lunches, late night live comedy shows—while also initiating my house hunt. The next day I reported back to work. I took the flak for my unexplained leave of absence, refused to give any explanations and just kept saying sorry for the inconvenience. My countenance betrayed my situation; I was behaving completely unlike myself. They probably realised that something was amiss. And yet not one of them pressurised me for an explanation. They were all warm and accepting. Soon it felt as though nothing had happened.

"I threw myself into my work. Took on everyone's on-call duties. It earned me a lot of brownie points. They were happy to give me time-off for house hunting.

"I found this real cute one bedroom about a kilometre from the workplace. Over the next month I got caught up in a whirlwind of making it my home."

Sonali continued after a pause, "Life settled into some semblance of order. Till about a month later when I started getting phone calls from Shubham's cousin. He tried to tell me how sorry Shubham was, how much he missed me, and all the emotional atyachaar (torture) that people generally use to manipulate you into doing what they want you to. I was like

'Okay. So why doesn't he make his own calls?' The fact was that I missed Shubham too, despite putting on a brave front. Something was definitely missing from my life. I desperately yearned for Shubham to call.

"Meanwhile, news that all was not well in my marital life had made it to the hospital. I suddenly started getting pitying glances from random people, looks that seemed to say, 'It's good that you are free now' and of course, wary looks.

"One day while I was discussing a case with Dr. Balbir I looked up to see Shubham staring at us. Dr. Balbir had caught me by the arm in a bid to stop me rushing off. I saw Shubham looking at us; he then turned on his heel and walked off.

"I fretted all day and cursed myself. But then, Shubham called me at night. He was real emotional. He kept saying, 'I am sorry. I love you. I miss you. Come back.'

"Having been where I had and back, I was not going to walk back into hell so easily. I told him that I was also missing him but we needed to sort things out first.

"Shubham lost his cool saying, 'I am telling you all this love you and miss you stuff that you crave and then you talk about sorting things out?' He hung up. The conversation had me more upset and puzzled than before. That night I could not sleep. What was wrong with me, why couldn't I just leave him? That got me wondering about whether it was the break-up that hurt me more or my ego. After all it is not nice to be thrown out of your own house."

She hesitated, as if she wanted to add something but then seemed to change her mind. She seemed to shake herself before continuing, "We landed up in the divorce court. I refused alimony or maintenance. I just wanted to be free of both of them; I wanted a clean break.

"I probably lived with the situation longer than I would otherwise have. I did not let my parents know what was happening.

"Retrospectively, I feel I should have kept in touch with my family and taken them into confidence. Somehow, I did not want to drag them into the mess and although they called regularly, I cited work pressures and long working hours as excuses for the times I did not return calls or seemed upset.

"Fortunately by the time things came to a head in my marriage, both my sisters were married. At least I did not let them down in that sense. My aunt Saroj is a fashion designer. She's widowed and has no issues in talking about matters like these. She offered me unconditional support and has been my closest friend through all my difficult times. She held my hand through the divorce proceedings as well."

She sighed, "Do you see the irony now? I loved, married, divorced, and am childless and I am also a renowned fertility specialist," she said with a pale, humourless smile. "In fact I always think the quote, 'God forces me to serve as a midwife and prevents me from giving birth (Socrates 470- 399 BC)', fits me to a T."

We just held hands, mutually comforting and understanding each other.

Realising that she had just relived her entire painful experience, my heart went out to her. I hugged her and asked her if she would like to sleep over. She refused. The sun had set. She wanted to spend some more time alone on Chowpatty.

"I am okay. Go ahead. We'll catch up."

The sky was clear, the stars twinkling like diamonds. As I walked home, I realised that I still was in the dark about one thing... Manju...

18

My morning schedule was crazy. The number of patients coming back for redo surgery seemed to have increased. Today we were operating on 17-year-old Niger who'd had two of his heart valves repaired at the age of eight and now needed to have them replaced by mechanical valves. The only thing that concerned Niger was whether he would be able to continue playing football while his mother, the poor lady, couldn't stop crying, wondering if her son would come out of this second heart surgery alive. Each of us has different priorities. Medicine is definitely more than just doing your job.

As I neared the operating theatre I saw Anita waiting with... Oh it was Amit! I did not recognise the kid; he looked really smart dressed in a blue collarless t-shirt, denim blues, and Nike shoes.

Amit had been in a road traffic accident with his father on the Pune Mumbai Highway a year-and-half ago. The duo had been driving back in their Swift when a fully loaded trailer had rammed into their car head on. Amit's father had died on the spot. Amit had suffered an injury to his lung and there had been a rupture of the junction where the food pipe meets the stomach. He had undergone multiple surgeries for the injuries. Each time he had landed up on a ventilator post-surgery. The result was that his windpipe had narrowed down to such an extent at one point that he was breathless even when sitting. Amit was just nine-years-old.

After much deliberation my surgeon had meticulously planned a way to remove the narrowed part of the windpipe and join the upper and lower parts together. He explained everything to Anita and Amit. Amit knew only one thing— he wanted to get better, cycle and play cricket! Anita had been extremely brave. Losing your husband and having to see your son through multiple surgeries and now this! Hat's off to her. She was extremely scared but very positive.

The surgeon operated and removed almost an inch of the windpipe. Amit was given a chin stitch, which meant that his chin was fixed with a stitch to the front of his chest. He needed to literally keep his head down for ten days. Never once did that kid complain. He went through it all with a smile. You would find him playing video games or reading whenever you looked in on him. I would go spend time with him when possible. In fact Amit had taken the trouble of teaching me the nuances of playing Angry Birds. He loved Scrabble and beat me everytime we played.

Anita of course was constantly by his side. She managed the whole show alone. They had no other family.

It had been three months since the surgery and Amit was cycling and playing cricket without a problem. He was a normal kid doing what normal kids do. Miracles do happen.

I hugged Anita. They had come in to see me. Amit had painted me a lovely card. It's patients like him that ensure that you never stop believing in miracles. Meeting them restored both my mood and faith.

The medical profession sometimes feels like a roller-coaster ride. One moment you curse your life and luck and the next moment you look around and realise that you actually have it quite good and have no business complaining. While you complain that life is too bound by routine, the gentleman in ICU and his family are praying for life to get back to routine.

As I went about preparing my anesthesia end for the surgery, I couldn't help thinking how one complains about your personal needs not being met; like being able to go on a holiday, spend more time doing other things you like to do or buy that dress that you have been dreaming about, is not happening and realise that the good Lord has more pressing needs to take care off. Moral of the story, Anuja: quit complaining and save the"the "asking" for when you need something urgently. Else just take time off to thank Him.

The morning lived up to its expectation of being crazy. Niger's surgery took all of eight hours. Everything went as per plan. Thankfully, I could tell Rose that her son was going to be fine. I had just finished talking to an extremely grateful mother when my OT technician came running to me with my phone, "Madam, urgent call."

"Hello?"

"Anuja, Charles here, I have found my son." His voice was breaking, he seemed excited all right, but not thrilled, I couldn't tell if it was Charles or the signal." Anuja, an acquaintance called. I am going to meet Alex II," he said. After an embarrassed pause he added,"I know this sounds crazy, but could you also join us?"

"What?

"I thought possibly over the weekend, I would be grateful."

"Where?"

"Alex II is in Lucknow."

"Lucknow?"

"Will you come? It's important."

He seemed to be struggling with words and surprisingly, despite finding his son who had been missing for over a year, he sounded quite low. I found myself accepting his request, which seemed to relieve Charles.

"I will make all the reservations and call you. You will be picked up every step of the way, door-to-door delivery, so don't worry about any details, just pack."

After a pause he said, "Thanks, it means a lot."

My head was spinning. Charles should have sounded ecstatic at finding his son, instead he sounded sad. My friends had me on a roller-coaster ride that didn't seem to have an end.

I called Sonali and told her that I would be out for the weekend without going into the details. I called up Forum Hospital and apologised for having to cancel my meeting, promising to get back to them with a probable alternative date and then I hung up.

While I was on the phone, I decided to call Raghu. "Hi, how are you? What are you up to?"

"Hi stranger, where have you been? "

Talking to Raghu was always a pleasure. We made some small talk and spoke about our busy schedules. He had to do a lot of travelling in the week ahead. He was trying to decide between the offers he was receiving. Mumbai still seemed to attract him the most. Whatever his state-of-mind he always made you feel as if you were the only thing important to him. Something in me stirred.

"Oh no, you don't," I thought to myself. Don't get emotionally involved Anju!

19

I was to travel by the Indian Airlines at 9 am on Saturday morning. I tried to read, but found myself thinking of how life was anything but predictable. After my talk with Charles, I could only guess at what he had gone through.

I found myself thinking of my parents. I really missed them. I worried about them. I had contemplated moving back to Pune to be with them. Dad had rubbished any such thoughts and insisted that he needed a place to come to if he got tired of Mom's nagging. All this with a wink. The two were inseparable. The last time, I spoke to Dad I thought he sounded a little down. I needed to make a trip home at the earliest.

I was picked up and whisked to the airport in a black Mercedes. The driver met me at my door, escorted me to the check-in counter and through security. I travelled business class to Lucknow; talk about doing things in style! I picked my meal, stretched out, and chilled. I enjoyed the luxury.

I had a placard with my name on it being waved in my direction at the arrival gate when I reached. Charles had me booked at the Taj. A BMW took me to my destination. It was my first visit to Lucknow. The weather was cool and the cleanliness of the city really struck me. The roads I travelled were broad with separate cycling tracks, a far cry from Mumbai.

I received a warm welcome at the hotel; the suite I was escorted to was real cosy. "Well, girl," I thought, "you seem to have got yourself a nice five-star holiday. Enjoy it."

I took a leisurely shower. Just as I was settling down in front of the idiot box, the receptionist called me with a message from Charles, to say that we would be lunching at one. He also mentioned that a table for three had been booked.

Three? Probably Alex II.

Well, what I was wearing would do just fine-a peacock blue shirt and jeans. I had just enough time to do my hair and make it to the dining room.

Charles was waiting for me, smartly dressed in casuals. He looked worried, his face drawn and shoulders hunched like a man carrying the burden of the universe. He pecked me on the cheek and pulled a chair out for me to sit on. Just as I was seated, Charles got distracted by the arrival of someone at the door. I had my back to it so I didn't know who it was.

The next thing I knew Charles was escorting a salt and peppered, portly, mustachioed gentleman to the table. I shook my head; this was definitely not his son.

I was perplexed. What was going on? Why was he being so mysterious? First he had told me that he'd found his son and that I, who had just reconnected with him a month ago, must come to Lucknow, and now there was this gentleman.

That was resolved soon enough. Charles introduced him as Dr. Sharma. He was the head of the ICU and the Department of Anaesthesiology at Sagar Institute of Medical Sciences.

So... That still didn't explain anything.

I smiled at Dr. Sharma and shook hands, "Dr. Anuja…"

Charles was more effusive, "Dr. Anuja is a very close friend and a big support to me. Having her here means a lot to me." I gave Charles a funny look.

We exchanged pleasantries. The drinks were ordered. We settled down with our drinks-- beer for the guys and sweet lime with water for me. Dr. Sharma and Charles were discussing common acquaintances.

Charles turned to me. "Anuja you must be wondering why I dragged you all the way here. I need your help." He turned to Dr. Sharma, "Jayant, why don't you tell her, I am still finding it difficult to discuss it."

Dr. Jayant Sharma obliged, "I met Alex II on my last visit to the US. Imagine my surprise and horror when a hit and run victim, who resembled Alex II was brought in the day before. He was admitted in a state of unconsciousness with a head injury, multiple fractures and his identity was registered as 'unknown'.

"How Alex II came to be here is a mystery. Fortuitously, Charles had been calling up all his Indian acquaintances just in case Alex got in touch with any of them. In fact Alex had been particularly taken by the stories that I had told him about Lucknow and expressed his desire to visit me. Anyway, first I received a call from Charles asking me to keep an eye out for his son and then this unknown kid was brought in who strongly resembles Alex. So I called Charles. He flew in straight away and confirmed his identity.

"Alex II is a real fighter, he has suffered fractures in his right arm and his left femur which have been fixed surgically. He is still on the ventilator but is neurologically fine. We plan to wean him over the weekend."

Poor Charles. He must have been devastated. That explained the bags under his eyes and the reason he looked so stressed out. My heart went out to him. I covered his hand with mine. Charles, though extremely grateful for all the excellent medical care that his son had received, wanted to shift Alex II to Mumbai.

We decided to go to the ICU after lunch. None of us was very hungry and decided on some soup and sandwiches. The ride to the hospital was completed in silence. Each of us was taken up with our own thoughts. Sigh, there is no such thing as a perfect life. The only thing certain about life is uncertainty. I took Charles' hand in mine and squeezed it.

The hospital was state-of-the-art; well-equipped and staffed with extremely qualified and dedicated individuals. It's funny that even after spending most of your life in and around hospitals the unmistakable smell of antiseptic always hits you as you enter.

When I reached the ICU cubicle in which Alex II was, I paused at the door and observed the person lying on the bed—a strapping, muscular youth with a head full of pitch black hair. And yet his face betrayed a boyish innocence that belied his overall appearance. He had a wan look about him that tugged at your heartstrings.

His right hand and left leg were in plaster and he was hooked to a Siemens 900C ventilator. The only sounds in the cubicle were the beeps from the monitor keeping track of his heartbeat, "beep, beep..." and the rhythmic whooshing sound of the ventilator. Alex was on sedation and peacefully asleep.

All his parameters were stable, all his scores normal. There was no sign of any infection; he was on his way to recovery. After reviewing all the medical parameters I agreed with Dr. Sharma that an attempt to wean Alex II off the ventilator was in order.

However, we decided on a wait-and-watch policy when it came to the transfer to Mumbai. Alex II was doing well and attempting to move him now did not seem like a good idea. With Dr. Sharma he was in good hands. We could monitor the situation and decide on shifting him once he recovered a little more.

Having assured Charles that Alex II was in good hands and promising to organise everything at my hospital to shift him once he had settled down, we returned to the hotel.

I was to return to Mumbai the very next day—Sunday afternoon. I couldn't wait to get back. The Lucknow trip had left me melancholic. Definitely not like anything I had imagined. The journey back was uneventful and unfortunately gave me a lot of time to think.

20

Even domestic travel results in a change in one's time zone. I was home at three in the afternoon and I had precisely three hours of a working Sunday to prepare for the week ahead.

On my agenda: a general clean-up, a load of clothes in the washing machine, a change of linen, stocking up on groceries... Oh, oh! I was out of eggs and bread, my staple diet. There was just an hour left before the supermarket around the corner closed on Sunday. Grumbling, I pulled on my shoes and socks; forget about changing clothes, the jeans and T-shirt would do. It was around the corner, just to pick up bread and eggs.

Visiting the supermarket always leaves a huge dent in my wallet. You always end up with creams that you never use, packs that find their way into the dustbin after their expiry date, not to mention the high calorie chocolates (I am a chocoholic), cheese singles, muesli, plum cake, etc.

"I am sorry," I said absentmindedly to someone standing in front of me. I was so engrossed in checking out the products on the shelves that I had bumped into... Raghu? "Hi Raghu", I said, my heart jumping out of my chest, "What brings you here?"

"I was sort of hoping to bump into you," he said. "Oh!" I said.

"Charles called me and told me what a rock you had been to him. Not changed much have you; always available with a shoulder for someone to cry on."

"Yeah sure, how about providing me a nice broad shoulder once in a while," I thought. Feeling sorry for yourself eh, Anuja.

Frankly squirming under all the praise, I said cheekily, "Okay, so you were looking for me, do you need a shoulder too?"

The moment I said it I kicked myself, why do I always have to sound so aggressive, why can't I be all sweet and sugary instead?

Raghu laughed, "Miss Ice Maiden," he said calling me by my college nickname, which I hated. "I don't need a shoulder, just some company; affable company to be precise."

"Why don't we drop off the stuff and go for a walk?"

I paid the bill and was thankful for Raghu's assistance.

Carrying five loaded bags back would have killed me.

Even Raghu raised his eyebrows, "Enough to feed an army..."

Raghu refused my offer of coffee, handed the bags to the lift boy and offered to wait downstairs for me. I dumped the stuff on my dining table, gave the washing machine, which had just pinged its completion of a wash-rinse-spin cycle, a dirty look and walked out. I hurried down the steps two at a time.

I stopped in my tracks. Raghu had engaged the watchman in a conversation and he looked oh so... handsome.

The walk was real nice; cool breeze, fewer people, relaxing company. The sky was clear. We spent a lovely evening sitting on the Marine Drive promenade sharing a hot corn-on-the-cob with butter, a cutting chai followed by some chilly ice cream at Bachelors.

Just then Raghu's phone pinged with a message. He read it and turned to me.

"Anuja, you remember Constable Ram?"

How could I forget him; five foot seven, burly, paunchy, moustache that curled up at the edges, paan stained lips, gung-ho attitude, twirling his baton incessantly.

The first time I met Constable Ram was firmly etched in my memory. It was our final year. Raghu and I were in the same place for our surgical posting. It was around eight in the evening. The day had been hectic. We'd taken care of a couple of hernias, hydrocoeles, a thyroidectomy, an appendicectomy and a perforation. Later that day we had scrubbed out of the theatre and were heading for a coffee. We had been paged from the Casualty ward en route. Both of us had groaned. Casualty calls meant that it was an emergency, which translates into a possible surgery, which basically meant no coffee.

It was probably a trauma or an accident. We changed direction and headed to the Casualty, situated on the ground floor, which was bustling with activity as usual. The Casualty here does not resemble what one sees on Gray's Anatomy. Far from it, there are peeling walls, stained bed sheets, iron beds and well, chaos reigns. As suspected it was an accident. Unfortunately, the patient was brought dead and there was not much we could do. Just as we finished the formalities, a lady was rolled on a stretcher, followed by almost eight to ten people talking at the top of their voices. The Casualty quickly filled up with the unmistakable smell of burnt human flesh. The lady in the stretcher looked to be in her twenties with a pretty face. From her neck down her body was burnt, her flesh red and raw. Some patches of her skin were peeling off. She had weeping areas that were covered in blisters and blackened areas where the burn injury was the most severe. We leapt into action: resuscitating the patient, getting intravenous access, starting fluids, ascertaining the extent of burns, and assessing the extent of injuries. The girl was slipping in and out of consciousness. She was immediately shifted to the burns ward. Her diagnosis: 90 per cent burns. Radha, that was her name, in her pain- induced delirium kept saying, "Mala naka maru" (don't kill me). After settling her as best as we could, we went back to the Casualty to finish the formalities. It was a medico-legal case and there was a mountain of paper work that needed to be done. The group who had accompanied her came rushing across to talk to us. This was followed by a barrage of questions and abuses; "Kashi ahe?" (How is she?) "Maroon takla tila" (They have killed her). It was apparently a case of dowry burning. I was shocked. How could one human being actually murder someone in this horrendous manner? What did it take to commit an act so full of hate and malice? Even thinking about it gave me the creeps. In the midst of this chaos, Constable Ram walked in, chewing tobacco, strutting and spinning his baton.

Raghu spoke to him and told him that it was a clear case of attempted murder by burning. The constable looked at him with a sneer, "Nonsense. I have spoken to the family. It was an accident. The stove burst while she was making tea." Raghu was livid. From the mutterings of Radha and the stories of those accompanying her it did not sound "accidental" at all, more like homicidal.

We really did everything we could for Radha. She was in great pain. We dressed her wounds regularly, spent time with her. She refused to talk about what had happened. We tried hard to make her talk, tell us what had happened, but she would clam up. Her parents who were farm hands came after two days. It was as if she had pulled on just so that she could see them. She died within an hour of their arrival.

Her parents were heartbroken and inconsolable.

Her father started banging his head against the wall. We tried to console him, "Saheb, paise nahit tar porgi nako." (If you do not have money you should not birth a daughter)."

Radha had been married just two months. Her parents had initially agreed to the dowry demands made by her in-laws: cash, gold and a Bajaj scooter. The couple had ensured a good education for their only daughter. She was a Montessori school teacher. They had sold what little they had to ensure that she got an educated husband-a bank officer, and they had hoped for a better life for her; every parent's dream. After the wedding the demands increased else, they were told, their daughter would be sent back to their house for good.

The in-laws only came to the hospital on the day that Radha died. They actually seemed relieved at her death. Constable Ram had managed the statements in such a way that it read accidental death. Radha's parents did not want to press charges, they did not have enough money to feed themselves, forget hiring a lawyer. "We have lost our daughter, what will we gain by going to court now."

Raghu tried to talk to Constable Ram, tried to reason with him. "These people need to be punished. Some other girl will suffer at their hands. It could be your daughter tomorrow."

Constable Ram was both blind and deaf to the pleas, he took offence at the personal reference and refused to see or hear our appeal. He was definitely being paid under the table for his efforts. He had probably taken cash or kind from the boy's family to bury the case, literally.

Raghu saw that I had vivid memories of the event. Even thinking of the day brought back the smell of burnt human skin and gave me the goosebumps. In fact, I had consciously moved away from burn cases after that posting.

"After that day, I bumped into Constable Ram in the last semester of my Anaesthesia residency a couple of years later. It was another day of Casualty duty. I had been called in to resuscitate a patient. Halfway through, there was a flurry of activity at the door. Constable Ram burst in carrying a young girl in his arms, yelling, screaming and shouting, 'Someone help her'. His hands and face were black and his clothes bloody."

Raghu looked pensive. "We took the girl from him and put her on the casualty cot. She was beyond our care, dead. Our eyes locked, Constable Ram was in deep shock, that look conveyed everything. The constable crumpled, just collapsed on the floor and cried and cried, 'Maroon takli tila' (They killed her). 'Saheb mala maaf kara.' (Sir, please forgive me).

"His only daughter, burnt for dowry".

I just stared at Raghu, stunned... Was it divine justice?

Raghu shook himself mentally, "Constable Ram, changed that very instant. He put in his papers, resigned from the force and now actually spends all his time and energy trying to raise awareness levels about the evils of dowry and trying to counsel those who insist on both taking and giving it.

"And if you are wondering why I am telling you this story, it was because I was asked to convey a message from Constable Ram who is trying to rope me in on his anti-dowry campaign. He was remembering pretty Anuja madam. He was thrilled to know you are also here in Mumbai and he will be coming to the hospital to meet you. He wants us both to speak at one of his rallies."

We sat on Marine Drive for a while in pensive silence. Raghu was meeting the director of Forum for dinner. He dropped me off at my building gate. Not all our past memories were pleasant, it was worth reliving them if only to spend time with Raghu, alone. Something to cherish. The evening had been a dream.

I finished my mundane chores, sorting my shopping, cleaning up. Without realising it I had drifted off to sleep still on cloud nine.

I was up bright and early and awoke with a smile still on my face. No rings-alarm clocks or otherwise. I hugged my pillow, completely content. I felt truly refreshed. Maybe I needed more of this companionship. I actually had time for a leisurely shower, a good breakfast and surprise, surprise even to read the newspaper cover to cover and still make it to the hospital on time.

"You have a message". Trust my cell to break my reverie.

It was from Raghu, "Thanks for a lovely evening. Want to spend more time together." Yippee...

"You have a message". It was Sonali. "Missed you on the weekend. Thanks for everything."

"You have a message." From Charles this time. "Thanks for being there. Alex is better physically. He is off the ventilator and although he has not spoken yet he has at least started responding."

Wow, it was Thanksgiving Day. I was glad that my being there made my friends feel better.

Charles and Alex II were on the top of my mind. My heart really went out to both of them. I was praying really hard that Alex II would recover fast and that father and son would resolve their differences.

I called Dr. Sharma. "Dr. Anuja, Alex II is medically fine. We have managed to wean him off the ventilator."

"However..." now what, "Since removal of his breathing tube, he is listless, in a trance-like state. He refuses to communicate, refuses to eat. Charles is at his wits end, poor man.

"We've had the neurological team examine him. They confirmed that he doesn't have an anatomical problem. They are putting his refusal to communicate down to a case of post traumatic shock."

I thanked him for all the inputs and called Charles.

I caught him at a bad time, he broke down the moment he heard my voice, "Anuja, Alex..."

"Charles, just hang in there. We know that Alex is going to be just fine. Complete recovery may take a little time, but I promise you he will be fine." Playing God Anuja!

"I have spoken to Dr. Sharma. Why don't I come down again this weekend and we'll re-evaluate the situation and decide when we can shift him to Mumbai."

Charles seemed to have gathered himself; the thought of being able to do something positive seemed to help.

'I wanted to suggest it but did not want to push you. Would you please come?'

"Charles can I ever refuse you?" The only person who knew how I felt about Raghu and bailed me out of tight situations in college. The shoulder I cried on the day Raghu got married. Charles had been my rock throughout my toughest times in college.

"I will arrange everything. Just pack. Waiting for you. And Anuja, thanks..." so saying he signed off.

21

Before I knew it, it was Saturday morning and I was in Lucknow. I received the same five-star treatment. I had told Charles that I would make my own arrangements but he had insisted. We agreed to meet him at the hospital.

I quickly settled in, had a quick masala chai and headed to the hospital. I had called up Dr. Sharma and found him waiting for me at the reception.

We shook hands. "Dr. Anuja, Charles was so happy when you said you would come."

He took me to his consulting room and gave me a seat. "For all practical purposes Alex is alright. All his parameters are normal and all his tests are good. However, he is listless and refuses to communicate. He has not spoken a word, expressed no pain, no emotion, nothing. It is as if he has no will to do anything.

"Charles has been standing vigil at his bedside throughout. I have had to have him forcibly evicted on occasion. He has become a shadow of himself.

"Charles is taking it very badly. He has tried every possible trick to make Alex react. All he gets for his efforts is a blank look."

I thanked him and proceeded to the ICU. Alex II was sleeping. The monitor was recording his steady heartbeats, "Beep, beep..." his oxygen levels looked good as did his blood pressure. No ventilator, no urinary catheter. He definitely looked better.

Charles was sitting by his bedside, holding his hand. He had silent tears rolling down his cheeks and seemed to be praying.

I felt a lump in my throat. I entered and put my hand on his shoulder, wiping his tears when he looked up. He clung to me like a lost child. Minutes passed before Charles calmed down.

I touched my finger to my lips, gently gesturing to him to follow me. I took him to the cafeteria for a strong coffee and forced some hot buttered toast on him.

"It's a nightmare."

"Nightmares pass. Alex has recovered so well, he has had to deal with a lot, both emotionally and physically, he is a fighter. We'll have him back, as good as new."

Charles gave me a wan look and smiled weakly, "Now you know why I called you."

We returned to the ICU to find Alex sitting up in bed, a motherly matron trying to coax some hospital food on him.

I held his good hand and said, "Hi Alex, I am Dr. Anuja, How are you?"

No response.

The food tray had the usual hospital fair, khichadi, chapati, some salad, curd, dal and... ugh! karela (bitter gourd).

"Matron, if you really want him to eat, maybe we need some tastier food and a younger pretty someone to do the coaxing."

Everyone smiled, but Alex gave no response.

We left the matron to her endeavours and met up with Dr. Sharma. It was decided to wait a week before shifting Alex. Depending on the progress we would take a call about whether he needed further hospitalisation or whether taking him home while simultaneously arranging for a live-in nurse would make more sense.

I spent the day at the hospital with Charles. I packed him off for a much-needed shave and freshening up and insisted on him downing a hot bowl of soup and a full meal.

My morning flight was cancelled and rescheduled for the evening. That too got delayed because of a technical snag. I had already said my goodbyes and had two hours to spare. Being a Sunday the shops were closed. My driver suggested a visit to the Bada Imam Khana.

As cautioned by the driver I picked up a guide from inside the complex and spent a very historical hour. The stories attached to the old monuments are amazing. Apparently the place took eleven years to build (1773-1784). Those were difficult times. The Nawab wanted to ensure that everyone got a chance to earn a livelihood. He used to have the construction done by the poor in the daytime; and the rich who did not like to be seen working during the day razed it down by night. Both got paid, ensuring that everyone in the kingdom earned a livelihood!

The Bhool Bhulaiya was amazing! It was a maze. Every time one came to a crossing of four paths, one had to choose the right path or one could end up being lost deep in the bowels of the palace. But for my guide, I wouldn't have made it back in time for my flight.

I had just enough time for some trinket shopping before catching the flight. The little time spent sightseeing made me feel as if I had taken a holiday and gave me historical food for thought... elephants had been used to test the roof tops, the building had been built in such a way that anyone entering could be unobtrusively observed... the walls were adorned with 220- year old Belgian mirrors to help reflect the light of diyas thus magnifying their effect. Amazing!

My flight was scheduled to leave at 8:30 pm. I was at the airport at exactly 7:30 pm.

22

I had been unable to get in touch with Raghu and was actually suffering from withdrawal symptoms. For the first time in my life I understood, no experienced, the word yearning. I couldn't wait to meet him again.

Lost in my thoughts, I was already at the check-in counter. The elderly gentleman just ahead of me was enquiring about the status of the flight I was supposed to board. Apparently the flight from Delhi had not yet landed.

"Sir, the flight has been boarded but hasn't departed."

I groaned. It was going to be a long haul. Thank God I had my laptop handy. I cleared security and was amazed at the number of people waiting in the holding area. I managed to find a seat and settled down to work, only to emerge an hour later when the battery almost died on me and I realised that I had checked in my charger.

I turned off my system. By now the holding area was overflowing, all the flights seemed to be delayed. To make matters worse the air conditioner seemed to be switched off, and the food counter seemed to be getting emptied.

The overhead speaker crackled to life. "Passengers travelling on flight number C564 please note that the flight has been delayed by one-and-a-half hours; any inconvenience caused is deeply regretted."

Realising that I was thirsty and the flight was definitely delayed I got up to get a Bisleri. And of course after that there was no place to sit; so I started pacing the lounge.

Among the crowd were a group of dental students returning from a conference; a nineteen-something girl, dressed to kill, fanning herself with a magazine; a single mother travelling with her infant twins and a seven-year-old; and two or three groups of people with a look that seemed to say, "We are so excited that we are going to phoren!" They were wearing jeans, tight t-shirts (irrespective of their size and shape), leather jackets, shoes, hats and scarves and had tons of luggage.

No more announcements were made. The only eating joint in the place had shut down. All the other flights except ours had departed. The air conditioning had definitely been switched off. Children were bawling and everyone had started getting restless. Just as the decibel levels reached unbearable proportions, eureka! The flight landed. Everyone relaxed. We would be off in another hour at least. Even before the announcement, the line to board the flight was in place.

Forty-five minutes later we heard a gentleman who had been escorted outside the glass doors with his mother on a wheelchair bellowing at the airline staff.

"Technical snag", "Flight won't take off ", "The old man is going to have a cardiac arrest; he's so upset!" Snatches of his conversation travelled like Chinese whispers down the line. That was the last straw, the last semblance of a line went out of the window. It was a frenzy after that. The airport staff were mobbed and threatened before we were finally informed that apparently the flight while landing had damaged a wheel; 9:45 pm and counting.

All hell broke loose. Some people, like me, cancelled their boarding passes and started making alternative arrangements. The airport is totally cutoff. There was no transportation available at that time of the night and of course for those of us from out of town finding accommodation was a pain.

Even as I was trying to organise a ticket for the next day, news came to me that those who had not left the security area had pressurised the airlines into giving them an alternative flight out of the city. An announcement proclaimed that a flight would arrive from Mumbai by 1 am and depart half an hour later. A loud cheer went up.

I had spoken to Charles and his driver was on the way. Others had called taxis and booked hotel rooms...I called up Charles and told him of the new developments and told him not to worry and that I would call the next morning.

The second boarding pass was now being issued.

I decided to enjoy the situation since I couldn't change it, and started mingling and striking up conversations with my fellow travellers—kindred souls bound by distress.

I finally settled down on a seat near the dental students after a short wait. It was as though the passengers were playing a game of musical chairs—the seat one vacated was instantly occupied by another. The students seemed reluctant to move their conversation beyond tummy tucks, diet fads and "bad" in-laws.

I got into a conversation with a group of IVF specialists who were returning after a conference. Apparently the gentleman had a patient coming in at nine the next morning from Abu Dhabi to have her eggs harvested.

Another gentleman was travelling by air for the first time in his life. He was reporting for his first job ever. All his colleagues had travelled by train and actually collected money to pay for his ticket. He was extremely excited as well as nervous. Poor guy had been booked on a flight that had been rescheduled, forcing him to rebook on our flight. And now with all the snags, he was really upset and wondering whether he would actually ever get a chance to travel by air at all.

Come quarter-past one and we realised that our rescue flight had not left Mumbai; the pilots had refused to fly. An Avro was expected to arrive with spare parts.

But, now what? We were stranded. There was pandemonium in the waiting lounge once again. Even the senior citizens who had been maintaining a stoic, philosophical silence started vocalising their displeasure. Under duress, the airline organised rooms and transport for us. It was also decided to accommodate all of us on the regular morning flight while passengers booked on that flight with confirmed reservations would have their flight delayed for "technical" reasons.

We were "unchecked" again and boarded buses, cars, and taxis-whatever the airlines could arrange-and transported to different destinations.

We checked into hotels at 3:30 am and we had to check in at the airport by 6:30 am! I nevertheless sent up many prayers in thanks for the two-hour reprieve I had been given.

I showered and freshened up by 6 am. I was duly issued my third boarding pass in twelve hours for the same flight.

While boarding, we could see the repair crew working on the damaged wheel even as we took off at 9 am. I felt sorry for the passengers who would re-live our drama of the previous night .

23

Back to Mumbai, back to reality. I took a cab straight to the hospital. My cabbie was in a talkative mood. In spite of the tiring day before, I let him talk; in fact I started asking him how long he had been in Mumbai and where he lived.

What I received was an education in finance. The guy had been in Mumbai just seven years. He owned three cabs and already owned a one room flat at Saki Naka where he stayed; a one bedroom in Nerul, which he had rented out; and he had booked a two BHK in Panvel. He had two kids in the third and fifth standard, both went to private, English medium schools and as he proudly told me, he could also afford private tuitions for them.

Amazing! I joked, "Bhaiya, I have been in Mumbai 15 years and I can't afford a house here."

He went all serious on me and said, "Madam, that's because you don't save." That really made me sit up; it's not something you expect to be told by a taxi guy. "Huh?"

He continued without a break, "For example. How much do you spend on a cab every day? Say approximately hundred rupees. Multiply that into thirty and then into twelve and finally into the number of years you have been staying in Mumbai. See, you could have saved all that money if you had used public transport. There are always cheaper ways of doing things here. With all the money you could have saved, you would have been able to buy property in Mumbai. Then again... you could also have taken a loan against the capital and invested it—like we do-in a vehicle that we then rent out, a shop or a house."

Fait accompli. Whew! This guy should have been my CA.

I got to the hospital in forty minutes flat. I tipped the guy generously for the speed and his advice. I only got a look that said, "Ma'am you will never be able to afford a house in Mumbai".

The day was hectic; two bypass surgeries followed by a mitral valve replacement. It was past midnight by the time I got home. I fell on my bed and passed out from exhaustion and was just entering the land of the dead when I was rudely interrupted... "ring ring..." It was one in the morning! Groan. Not an emergency please!

"Hello," I said groggily.

It was Raghu. "Hi, what are you doing? I couldn't sleep so I decided to call?"

Talk about silly questions. What could I possibly be doing at one in the morning? I was not in a mood for conversation even with Raghu. If he couldn't sleep what was I supposed to do? Sing him a lullaby? Grr...

I cursed all the mobile service providers for their night schemes; call friends at low costs so you can ruin their night's sleep.

"Hey, I hope I did not disturb you," he said and when my reply was less than affectionate he added with consternation, "Sorry, will call tomorrow."

Oh no, you don't. I was wide awake now. After all it was Raghu.

"No, no, no problem at all. What's up?"

"I met Charles today. He tried to call you, your cell was switched off."

"Oh yes, I was operating with a hyperactive surgeon today. He gets upset if anyone on the team receives or makes calls. It's safest to keep it switched off."

"Charles has taken the evening flight back. He's one dedicated father. Alex is recovering well. Did you know that Charles and Sonali had actually been sweethearts in Delhi? He had actually proposed to her? Has Sonali told you anything about that?"

Groan... talk about being unromantic. At one thirty in the morning I definitely expected something more than a post mortem on a Charles and Sonali love affair, that I did not even know existed. And why was Raghu so worked up about it? Enough to call me at such an unearthly hour? Nevertheless, I felt myself starting to wake up. "No Anuja. Don't give in to temptation. You have a long day tomorrow," I thought.

"Raghu, why don't we meet and catch up. I have had a long day and am really zapped."

We exchanged pleasantries and disconnected. My beauty sleep was really disturbed. I tossed and turned and finally drifted off into restless slumber only an hour or so later, with thoughts of Raghu, Charles, Sonali, Shubham and... Manju running through my head.

24

The entire week was a whirlwind of activity; I only managed short one minute conversations with Charles, Raghu, and Sonali. Charles was spending all his time at the hospital with Alex II, Raghu had gone to Surat to check out the possibility of starting up his own intensive care hospital and well, Sonali was in Delhi at a conference.

I actually had a day to myself bang in the middle of the week. There were no cases posted and I could just chill. I decided to take care of an article that I was to shoot off for a leading healthcare magazine. The deadline was still a week away, but it always helped to stay ahead.

I was continuing with my fitness regime. An early morning jog and hot shower later, I settled in to write the article. I was just getting warmed up when I realised that my phone had not rung since the evening before, which was very unusual.

A quick check revealed that my phone had gone into silent mode, and it showed that I had 22 missed calls! I'd got 12 in the last twenty minutes alone, from the OT, the recovery room, my senior surgeon and residents. Wondering at the panic I called up my senior surgeon.

"Kahan hain tu?" (Where are you?)

"We have been trying to get in touch with you frantically. We have a gunshot chest injury that needs to be taken up stat. It's on TV."

"I will be there in five minutes."

A gun-shot victim at 11:30 in the morning? I switched on the TV as I changed.

Apparently the general manager of a national bank had been shot. Shot by one of the bank security guards!

I made it to the hospital in ten. I was in the OT and in my scrubs in fifteen. While waiting for the patient to be wheeled in, the residents filled me in.

"Ma'am apparently the security guard had been on leave for ten days without giving any intimation to the bank. He came to work today morning, changed, collected his weapon and went to meet Mr. Chandra, the General Manager, to report back on duty. He informed Mr. Chandra that he had been unwell and hence had not come in.

"Apparently, the security guard was a known alcoholic. Mr. Chandra asked the guard to obtain a medical certificate from the doctor treating him and submit it to the HR department of the bank before rejoining. In a fit of anger, the guard had opened fire yelling, 'Ye rahan apka medical certificate' (here's your medical certificate).

"The general manager was hit in the chest. Without wasting a single minute he rushed out of his room, all the while bleeding profusely. With his hand over his chest, Mr. Chandra had walked down three floors, asked his guys to get him a taxi, since getting the bank car would take time and had them rush him to the hospital.

"Apparently, Mr. Chandra had made a list of all employees with alcoholic problems and passed a dictum that the salary cheques of these people would only be handed over to the spouse or family member of the person in question. The security guard had actually brought his wife to the bank to collect his cheque today. She had been waiting downstairs while the drama unfolded.

"The security guard had locked the door after Mr. Chandra had left the room. People heard a single shot behind the door. The guard shot himself. Even now his body is on its way for post mortem.

"Hats off to Mr. Chandra for his presence of mind. His staff were too shocked to even react; they sort of froze and were not sure about what was happening. He kept giving instructions and took charge of the situation himself despite taking a bullet."

Just then Mr. Chandra was wheeled in. The bandages around his chest were soaked and dripping with blood. He was hooked to an intravenous line and a unit of blood was already finding its way into his veins.

Mr. Chandra was not only coherent but also totally alert. He shook my hand as I introduced myself. He had the presence of mind to wish the entire surgical team best of luck as he was shifted to the operating table. I hooked him up to the monitors, and put in another large bore intravenous line as we talked. Within minutes the anaesthetic drugs took effect and he slipped into deep sleep. I quickly put in the other vascular accesses while the surgical team got into action.

The X-ray film showed that he had pellets embedded in different parts of his chest. The rifle fired was an old fashioned one which used cartridges with pellets, which were embedded in his muscle, bone, as well as in his abdomen. Mr. Chandra was extremely lucky. The bullet had hit the sixth rib on his right side and had missed injuring his lung, heart and other major vessels in the region. It had been deflected, travelled downwards, pierced the diaphragm, and actually ripped through the liver, although the bowels had not been injured.

The blood flowing out of the chest wound was actually tracking from the abdomen through the diaphragm to the skin wound. The surgeons got to work. Our blood bank had really come through. All our blood products were flowing in as asked for. We required all of five litres of blood and almost an equal amount of clotting factors.

The total surgical time was almost six hours. The diaphragm had to be reconstructed and the liver that was in rags was stitched together by the surgeons, using lots and lots of surgical glue. They retrieved as many pellets as possible before closing him up and declaring that all was well.

It was decided not to wake him up on the table. We would observe him overnight and only allow him to come around when everything else was stable.

We had all missed lunch and realised how ravenous we were only once we shifted and settled Mr. Chandra into his recovery room. Someone had ordered pizzas and chicken biryanis. The general surgical team and the cardiac team had worked together and were quite pleased with the outcome. We watched the news channels as we ate. Mr. Chandra's story was splashed all over. The media was having a field day. The details of the shoot-out were being played and replayed. They kept replaying gruesome scenes of the trail of blood left by Mr. Chandra on the staircase as he walked out of the bank, and shots of the guard's body as it was taken away for post mortem. Even his wife had not been spared. The poor lady was in a state of shock and unable to comprehend the turn of events. What really caught my eye was the look of confusion on the face of the bystanders in the bank. Even with all the terror attacks and calamities that we witness on a day-to-day basis, none of us is really equipped to handle such situations when we are right there in the thick of things.

We sat vigil over Mr. Chandra for another couple of hours. He had settled down, got his colour back and all his systems seemed to be working well.

I spoke to his wife; the poor lady was in total shock. After all she had sent her husband off to work hale-and-hearty that morning.

25

On Friday morning I called Dr. Sharma and spoke to him at length. He felt that Alex was now physically fit to travel. However, he also mentioned that Charles would prefer Alex to be shifted from ICU to ICU to ensure that everything stayed fine. It was decided to bring Alex over the next weekend and settle him into the ICU at my hospital.

Charles had purchased a sprawling two BHK apartment in Cuffe Parade the week before and was busy doing it up for Alex. Talk of the power of money. He had been shuttling between Lucknow and Mumbai to put the place together.

Finding myself at a loose end, I decided to surprise my parents by visiting them. I reached Pune on Saturday morning and I don't know who was more surprised. They had house guests and I was relegated to the diwan in the drawing room.

But wait; this is not to say that my parents weren't elated at my arrival. They did their usual fussing about how thin I looked and how I needed to be fed. All my favourite dishes were planned for breakfast, lunch and dinner over the next two days.

What made them uncomfortable was that the house guests were family friends and they had come with their daughter. Apparently, they had made a meet a prospective groom programme in the evening. They knew how averse I was to such events and feared my reaction.

I reassured them that as long as I was not the bride to be "seen" they could organise as many such programmes as they desired. In fact they were relieved when I actually started helping out with the arrangements.

The girl, Pooja, was a smart, sweet and pretty twenty-five-year-old. She was an airhostess in Taxila airlines and was doing extremely well for herself. It was another case of you-must-get-married-now pressure from her parents. Emotional atyachaar at its worst. Anyways she was okay with the whole dekho business. The guy she was meeting was a twenty-nine-year-old MBA settled in phoren.

It was all quite funny really. She'd received the same proposal when she was nineteen. At that time Pooja had refused to even see the guy as she wanted to finish her studies first. And for some reason the guy had not married yet. Then six months ago the same family approached Pooja for their younger son who was an IT graduate, also settled in the US. When Pooja learnt that they were in fact looking for girls for both the boys she asked to meet the elder one. She showed me the photograph; he was a handsome six-footer. I sighed enviously. Where were these guys when I was still in the business of "seeing" them?

Come evening and everyone got dressed. For once I obeyed my mom's request to wear a salwar kameez instead of my trousers, considering that it was someone else's prospects on line. The family came and so did the guy. The family was nice and all over Pooja. But the guy! He was half bald! They probably forgot to update the photograph they had sent Pooja. I saw Pooja's expression changed when she saw the guy, sorry Rahul, in person. The younger brother on the other hand, was a rock star.

Rahul, was head over heels in love with Pooja the moment he saw her. The family insisted on them going out together. The couple was back half-an-hour later. In their absence things were as good as finalised. I was like,"What? At least ask the girl!"

Anyway, after a lot of "We will meet at the earliest to finalise dates", the boy's side left. What followed was complete mayhem. Pooja was not happy with the match. The guy did not want her to work after marriage (where had I heard that before). She was not impressed by him at all. He was a mama's boy and the fact that he was balding did not help. Pooja was like, "If I have to dekho guys give me a perfect specimen".

Then started the coercing, "Beta acchi family hain (Child, the family is good). The people are nice. They will look after you. Finally, you must be comfortable with the family. After a few years all guys become bald. What would you have done if he became bald after marriage?"

It reminded me of what one of my aunt's used to insist on repeating, "Beta, never go by looks; all guys are rock stars once the lights go out."

Probably because of my presence my parents stayed out of the drama unfolding before us.

Meanwhile, I got an SOS from the hospital and had to cut my holiday short. Pooja stuck to her guns and got her way. "Better luck next time!" I thought chuckling to myself.

26

I was up to my eyebrows in work the whole week. As planned, I travelled to Lucknow on Saturday and accompanied the father and son duo back on Sunday. Alex had done well. The trip went without a hitch. We had wheelchairs readily available at both ends and with all of Charles' contacts we sailed through the all the formalities.

We took Alex directly to my ICU where all the necessary arrangements had been made. He was still in plaster. It would be another three weeks before they came off. He continued to be withdrawn; only answering in monosyllables when required. The rest of the time he maintained a blank look and stoic silence. He was a shadow of the energetic, lively youth I had been shown a photograph of.

We settled Alex in a cubicle. As we came out, Charles crumbled. There were tears rolling down his cheeks. I held him and took him to the doctors' room and gave him a glass of water.

"You are such a good father. He will be fine, don't worry." "Good father? You don't know the half of it. I really wonder what drives us as doctors. When our families are young we have heavy rotas and little money. We don't have time for them; we can't do everything we want for them. Getting ahead is difficult; we have to continuously prove ourselves. Even when a member of our own family is unwell, we have to leave them to attend to someone else."

On reflection I realised what he was saying was true. This is probably the one profession where to the patient you are"are "soulless" and "family less". You are not supposed to be on a holiday, take time off or be sick. You have to be available when he calls.

I remembered a colleague of mine, Ritu who was married and had a very understanding three-year-old. She was in a desperate situation one night. Her daughter was burning up with fever and she had been busy putting cold compresses on her forehead in the middle of the night when the ICU had called that a twenty-something youth who had been in an accident (he was speeding on his bike) had been brought in with head injuries and needed to be ventilated. Torn between her child and duty she had passed on the compresses to her husband and got up to leave. She knew the fever would subside but the youth could lose his life. As she was getting up her daughter held her nightdress and in her delirium she said, "Mama, every time you tell me someone is unwell and you have to go, today tell them that I am unwell and you can't come."

Medicine was a "noble profession" alright...

I was brought back to the present by Charles."Charles. "I could never make it for his matches. He was the captain of his school football team. He was also offered a sports scholarship," he said with a hint of pride and regret.

"He was a quiet kid. Invariably, whenever we sat down to talk, I would be called away. Slowly the time we spent together dwindled. Our conversations were to the point and crisp. Then, with Victoria's drinking problems and wild parties, our slanging matches and door banging, Alex became invisible, a not-seen, not-heard component of the house. Looking back, I do not know how many days he went to bed without food; or for that matter whether he was even home.

"From being a brilliant student, he started becoming an indifferent one. Victoria started taunting him; she was perpetually drunk and abusive those days. The last conversation I had with him was when he came home the night Victoria died."

Charles had a haunted look on his face as he recalled the moment, "Alex entered and found me cradling Victoria's body at the foot of the staircase. He went crazy, he took one look at us and started screaming, 'You killed her, you killed her. All you care about is yourself.'

"He had a wild look on his face, tears were streaming down his face as he turned and ran off into the night. I rushed out after him only to see the tail lights of his car disappearing into the distance. I was torn between following him and getting back to Victoria.

"I returned to the house and called the medics and the police. Alex stayed away from the house. He only came on the day of the funeral; no words were exchanged. The police interrogated him after the funeral. He told the police about our fights and also the suspicious conditions in which he had found me.

"The inquest was closed with a verdict of not guilty, but the shadow of her death still follows me.

"Alex had one of our family retainers take specific personal items to him. He never visited the house again. After much legwork I found out about his having travelled to India three months ago."

My heart went out to Charles. He seemed to have been chased by his demons all his life. I sent up a silent prayer for him.

"The whole episode forced me to rethink my priorities in life. I went from being an acclaimed cardiac surgeon to a murder suspect in seconds. I had no family, my own son considered me the murderer of his mother! That is when I decided to return to my roots. At least I have friends here. I am incidentally looking for options in Mumbai. I have to take a call. Maybe I will just put away everything in a trust for Alex. I am in the process of winding up my old life. Alex's accident has been a wake-up call. I want a cosy place where we can spend time together. I want to find my son again."

We sat in silence. I got us both a strong cup of coffee. By the time we finished, Charles had managed to reign in his emotions.

Raghu had also come in to see if there was anything he could do. We looked in on Alex who was sleeping and decided to call it a day. I packed Charles off after ordering him to get a good night's rest.

I sighed and put a hand over my tired eyes. I looked up to see Raghu watching me. There was tenderness and yearning in his eyes that I had never seen or experienced before. It was a magical moment. He started to put an arm around me, but guess he realized that we were standing in the middle of an ICU. We just smiled at each other. He took my hand.

"Can I drop my good lady home?"

My knight in shining armour… I was tempted to accept but was confused and still recovering from what I thought I had read in his eyes.

I shook my head and saw him off. I waited a full ten minutes to let my heart rate settle, before picking up my bag and heading for home. Maybe I should have accept his offer of a drop home. Maybe more magic would have happened tonight. Anuja, you are a coward. He loves me, he loves me not…

Iwas fresh the next morning, having slept surprisingly well. I decided to look in on Alex before going to the theatre. Imagine my surprise at finding both Raghu and Sonali at his bedside. Alex was actually smiling and holding Sonali's hand. Talk about progress.

Not wanting to disturb them, I left for my surgery - an ASD (Atrial Septal Defect, simply put—a small hole in the heart) that my surgeon made short work of. I was out in two hours. The next case was posted later in the afternoon.

I returned to the ICU to find Raghu visiting Alex II and making young hearts flip. He had apparently been waiting to meet me. Yippee!

We made our way to the cafeteria. We bumped into Zaks and Rekha as we entered. I saw Raghu giving Zaks, a quizzical look. Zaks never failed to draw a response. Tall, muscular, ponytailed, bespectacled, he cut quite a fine figure.

Zaks actually came from a family of sweet-makers and confectioners. The family had a roaring business and a huge manufacturing plant that made both mithis and munchies at Yavatmal. Zaks was ambitious. He did not want to join the family business and wanted to be known as more than a "sweet" man.

He was engaged to Dr. Rekha who was pursuing her postgraduate studies in Pathology. They were both from Yavatmal and sweethearts from medical college. The only reason they were in Mumbai was to be together. Apparently Zaks' family had reluctantly agreed to the match, but Dr. Rekha's parents were totally against it. Zaks was adamant that they would only marry with the approval of both their families or just wait it out. They had been going around for almost four years and were still hoping to convince Rekha's father. I thought it to be real sweet and unusual for someone to be so patient in today's day and age.

We had just settled down to our cuppas when Mr. Raj came looking for me. His ten-year-old son had been admitted for a dental procedure and since I was known to the family, they were insisting that I anaesthetise him for the procedure. Mr. Raj had called me up and told me that he needed to talk to me.

He came up to the table, "Ma'am..." he began, his expression changing when he saw Raghu who had got up to greet him. He mumbled a, "He's in 1405" and hurried away but not before throwing a dirty look in Raghu's direction.

I gave Raghu my trademark, "What's up" look. He shrugged and sat down.

"What was all that about? Do you know Mr. Raj?"

"He is from Pune remember, they own the famous Raj publishing house."

"Okay, the Pune connection... So what?"

Raghu ran his finger along the edge of his coffee cup, "Do you remember how it feels when you finish your specialisation and get into private practice? You feel like you can play God."

"Aie (mother) was admitted to Gokhale nursing home. It was a Sunday afternoon and I was visiting her.

"Mr. Raj brought his wife, who was in labour, to the nursing home. Dr. (Mrs.) Gokhale was her attending obstetrician. As luck would have it, Dr. Jha, her regular anaesthesiologist was away and Mrs. Raj needed a caesarean section. The child was in a transverse lie breech position with an extended head. There were signs of foetal distress and a caesarean section was imminent. I happened to be around. Both Dr. Gokhale and Mr. Raj knew me and requested me to do the honours.

"Like a good Samaritan I agreed.

"The spinal was perfect, everything was going well, that was well... till Dr. Gokhale made an incision on the uterus and introduced her hand.

"There was very little amniotic fluid and the uterus clamped down on Dr. Gokhale's hand. She was osteoporotic (a condition that weakens bone tissue and increases the risk of a broken bone). The poor lady actually fractured her index finger and dislocated her shoulder during the procedure."

"What!"

"Yeah, the baby was stuck. After a lot of pushing from my end and pulling from the other end, we managed to pull the baby out. The neonatologist had not arrived and I took charge of the baby who did not cry at first. I used suction to clear the airway before introducing an endotracheal tube and got the child to breathe. It was after we heard it cry that we heaved a sigh of relief. Three cheers went off in the theatre. Like a victor carrying his prize, I announced the arrival of the heir to the Raj fortunes to the family, holding the baby in my arms.

"A son... always a prized possession. From then on I was a favourite of the Raj household. Every time they met me I received effusive thanks. I was the guest of honour at the baby's naming ceremony. I was revered like God.

"Soon after, I moved out of Pune. The next time I returned I decided to visit the Raj household and reached there unannounced bearing presents for the child who was a little more than a year old.

"I rang the bell and was let in by an old family retainer who gave me a look that said,"Why have you come?" I was perplexed but ignored it. I was shown into the drawing room. Mr. Raj walked in after almost a quarter-of-an-hour and was not exactly happy to see me.

"Wondering at the coldness, I placed the gifts on the table and exchanged routine pleasantries. Mr. Raj offered me tea and coffee but his body language was hostile. I excused myself at the earliest and left.

"I later learnt that the child had probably suffered from hypoxic brain damage, which was now evident. From being WLG (worshipped like God) in the household I was now PNG (persona non grata)."

That was probably the reason why Mr. Raj was so paranoid about his son going under anaesthesia. I could only ponder over the dilemma of having an only son who was mentally challenged from what were considered "avoidable circumstances". Poor Raghu, he had done his best under the circumstances. If the delivery had been uneventful, if the neonatologist had made it in time. The ifs and buts of the event were never ending. We do our best, but sometimes the results of our actions are beyond our control and they come back to haunt us. Destiny and fate we bow to thee.

Raghu had to leave and I returned to my rounds. Having finished my surgical list early I decided to spend some 'me' time.

As, I was leaving the hospital premises I saw Zaks getting into an Anti-Terrorist Squad jeep. As I wondered at what Zak got up to in his free time, I got into a cab and headed for the beauty parlour.

28

The next morning saw me up early. A brisk walk and a spurt of running put me in a real good frame of mind. A hot cup of coffee in hand, I cuddled up on my sofa with a cushion resting on my knees and settled down to read the Mumbai Mirror.

I was so shocked when I read the headlines that I spilt my coffee. It read Munnabhai at Corporate Hospital and had a picture of Zaks staring back at me. "Dr. Akhtar Hussain alias Zaks, resident doctor at Corporate Hospital, arrested." The story ran into two pages.

Apparently, a gentleman from Zaks' hometown of Yavatmal had come to Mumbai and been introduced to Zaks. He returned to Yavatmal and met Dr. Akhtar Hussain, a resident doctor at Criticare Hospital, Yavatmal and mentioned that he had met his namesake at a Corporate Hospital in Mumbai who preferred to be called Zaks. Initially, Dr. Akhtar Hussain thought it to be a coincidence till he realised that the gentleman also shared his middle name. Considering this to be too much of a coincidence, he decided to investigate, especially since he remembered that he'd had a batch mate in the first year of medical college called Zaks who had dropped out. He came to Mumbai and realised that he was being impersonated by Zaks, who had assumed his identity and actually procured copies of his degree certificates!

It was enough to send him rushing to a police station to lodge a complaint.

The news really stunned me. Apparently, Zaks had done marginally well in the medial qualifying exams and persuaded his father to pay the capitation fees. He had been unable to cope. Having flunked thrice in the first year of medical college Zaks had dropped out. Unable to break the news at home, Zaks had continued to let his family believe that he was a doctor and had shifted to Mumbai to keep up the charade.

Zaks had been with the unit for over five years. He had actually been assisting in cardiac surgeries and was responsible for patient care. Since he was just a medical graduate working in a super specialty his work was always supervised.

The news had really shaken me. My thoughts kept returning to Zaks as I dressed and drove myself (for a change) to hospital. I still couldn't believe it. Zaks was a nice kid. Even medically he had performed and learnt faster than some of our "medical graduates". It was amazing how one could interact with a person for five years and still not know them at all.

As expected, the operation theatre was abuzz with the news. Some were shocked, the know-it-alls strutted around with an air that seemed to say, "We always knew there was something amiss with him" and then there were those who were playing up the religious angle of this incident. Zaks had been caught on the wrong foot.

As a result, our list started late. Our chief surgeon, a big man with an even bigger circle of connections, had been to see the Police Commissioner to enquire about Zaks. The Commissioner asked him to stay out of the matter since there seemed to be more to the whole affair. This was followed by a "damage control" meeting with the hospital's management.

The theatre list only consisted of an Atrial Septal Defect (hole in the heart) closure. During the procedure updates on Zaks kept trickling in.

"They have discovered a passport in the name of Dr. Akhtar Hussain with Zaks' details from his friend's hostel room.

"The police are in the operating room complex. They are here to check Zaks' lockers." Considering the nature of the problem we had on hand and the fact that our other resident was on leave, the Chief requested me to settle in and look after the post-operative ward till things settled down. He would take the surgical calls.

The ward was full. I had to call Raghu and cancel our dinner date. I was feeling like a heel for cancelling at the last moment till he mentioned, "Guess I will call up Sonali and catch up with her over dinner then." That really got to me. I cursed my luck. I could have murdered him. Damn, Raghu. Damn, Zaks.

29

I had my hands full, what with Alex in my hospital and the Zaks issue. The Police Inspector had been in and had been quizzing the doctors and the staff. None of us had anything to add and in fact were looking to him for the latest updates.

Raghu and Sonali became regular visitors to the hospital and really kept a vigil over Alex. Charles seemed to be holding up better with all the moral support he was getting. We all made sure he had his meals on time and bullied him to leave once visiting hours were over.

Interactions with Raghu and Sonali seemed to be helping Alex. In fact Sonali had started spending most of her time with Alex. She had managed to penetrate his defences and was actually able to strike up conversations with him. With everyone else the conversation was a monologue with the only inputs from Alex being "uh" and "ah".

Sonali started bringing Alex books, which he enjoyed, and also bought him an ipod loaded with what apparently were his all-time favourite songs. To top it all, she actually managed to feed him! Alex was definitely on the mend and getting stronger.

I cornered Sonali and had to ask her, "Sonali, have you really met Alex for the first time here in the hospital or do you know him from before?"

She laughed, "You'll never believe this. I have been playing agony aunt to this kid on Facebook over the last couple of years. I had been wondering why he had dropped off the networking site. His last post was about his plan to visit India, the land of his father."

I had to know more. I dragged Sonali to the cafeteria. "How did you manage to put two-and-two together?"

"Stupid question, these kids love posting their photos online."

I hit my forehead, "How stupid! Of course."

"You said you had been his agony aunt, what do you know about him?"

"All kids while growing up have lots of questions about the birds and the bees and there are not so right ways of getting in on the net. I use my website as a place where the kids can ask these questions freely and get answered in a more appropriate way. In the process some kids start writing in about some other issues that may be bothering them and connect on Facebook. In fact I am connected with quite a few kids who share their highs and lows with me.

"I obviously did not know that I was interacting with Charles' son. He never mentioned his parents, and finding out that he was Charles' son actually came as something of a shock.

"We became acquainted about two years ago. He sounded like a real rebel, but good at heart. His posts used to be bubbly yet soulful. He came across as a fun-loving, responsible kid with clear ideas about what he wanted out of life, though a little melancholic.

"Do you know that the kid actually pretended to do drugs so that his parents would take notice of him? He thought they would rally around him if they thought he needed them both.

"He has actually got a football scholarship to do his engineering. Poor kid got the news the morning his mother died."

"Sonali, has he mentioned how his mother died or the circumstances in which it happened?"

Sonali thought a bit, "The Facebook posts only indicated his loss and his emotions. There were no details. Soon after, he dropped off the radar. There were sporadic posts about his decision to postpone starting university after, as he said, 'he found himself'.

"Alex has been through a rough time, he wants to talk and I would rather he did it when he is ready. He is a good kid, down to earth, intelligent, caring. Charles must be proud of him."

I was happy for Charles. There was a silver lining to this story after all.

However, everytime Sonali mentioned Charles' there was a hint of sadness and frustration. It got me wondering about Raghu's late night call.

30

The morning promised to be hectic. I called ahead and asked the first patient to be called to the theatre. He needed an aortic valve replacement surgery; his heart valve was leaky.

I entered the theatre to find a new anaesthesiology resident there. Finding an anaesthesiology resident in the cardiac theatre is a novelty in itself. They normally have to be coerced to enter the cardiac theatre. The long hours are not everyone's cup of tea.

I sized her up. Young, cute, looked apprehensive; was more concerned about her hair getting mussed up under her scrub cap and her nails getting chipped while breaking the drug ampoules than what was happening around her. Dr. Alka Bannerjee, it appeared to be her first day in anaesthesiology; forget the cardiac theatre. I groaned mentally.

"Dr. Alka, since it is your first day, you can observe what I do and ask questions," I said.

She nodded and moved aside. I kept up a monologue explaining what I was doing as I went about my business of putting in the lines and beginning the procedure to put the patient under anaesthesia.

Everything went off smoothly. The patient was under and all draped and painted. The surgeons were in; the patient was now hooked up to the heart lung machine. I settled down to read my journal.

Suddenly, from the corner of my eye, I became aware of Dr. Alka becoming restless and agitated. I looked up and found her all worked up and red in the face.

"Dr. Alka, what's the matter?"

"Ma'am, why are you not doing anything? The patient is bleeding to death?"

Now, she had me in a spin, "Excuse me?"

"The patient's heart is draining out! There is no blood in the heart, the patient is dying," she said wringing her hands. She was getting hysterical.

The surgical team was giving us looks from over the screen.

Good thing the Chief was not scrubbed up yet.

I gave Dr. Alka a seat and proceeded to explain the concept of a heart-lung machine to her and exactly what the surgeons were going to do.

"Dr. Alka the surgeon needs to operate on the heart. The heart has to be empty and at rest while they work. The patient's blood is being diverted into the heart lung machine, which will pump the blood and oxygenate it, similar to the function performed by the heart and lung. Once the surgeons are done, we'll restart the heart, all the blood from the machine will be returned to it and everything will be as good as new."

Throughout the explanation, Dr. Alka was like a jack-in-the-box. She was too agitated to sit down.

"Dr. Alka if you are not comfortable, would you like to leave the theatre and come back after a cup of coffee, perhaps?"

"No ma'am I am okay. I will stay." "Are you sure?"

She nodded. Even after the detailed explanation she was not convinced and remained skeptical. "You mean the patient is technically dead."

How did one answer that? Technically dead?

The next thing I knew she had passed out on me! We lifted her out of the operating theatre onto a patient trolley. Chief had walked in as we were carrying Dr. Alka out. Never one to miss a chance at teasing us he said, "Never short of excitement, are we? Anaesthesized the new recruit, I see." as he saw me entering.

We wheeled her to the recovery room bed and resuscitated her. Once she came around she was still white. Asking her to rest, I called in one of her roommates and had her accompany Dr. Alka to their room once she felt better.

Apparently that was Dr. Alka Bannerjee's first and last day in the department of anaesthesiology. She decided that something like dermatology was all she could handle.

31

Sonali had been trying to get in touch with me. I called her once I settled my patient in the postoperative ICU and asked her to meet me for a much needed cuppa. After the Dr. Alka fiasco, I needed it badly. I pulled my apron over my scrubs and went out to join Sonali.

Sonali took one look at me and burst out laughing. That really upset me, "What's so funny?"

Sonali realised my mood, "Nothing, sweetheart you need a break."

As we settled down on the couch with our respective cuppas, Sonali said, "Alex finally opened up today." Now, she had my attention.

"Do you know what has really been bothering him?" I was all ears.

"He received the news about his engineering scholarship and college admission on the morning of his mother's death. He had no one at home to share the good news with. His grandfather was no more, his dad had left early for work and his mother was in a drunken stupor. His friends called him up and wanted to celebrate.

"He promised to meet them in the evening. For some reason that day he was not comfortable leaving his mother alone.

"He looked in on her at around nine and found her fast asleep. Charles had not returned from the hospital. Alex decided to step out for a bit. He kissed his sleeping mother and left.

"And when he returned he found his mother dead and his father standing over her.

"Alex feels responsible for her death. He keeps blaming himself. Keeps wondering if she would still be here if only he had stayed home... He is unable to make up his mind about his father's involvement in the whole thing.

"The last time he saw his father was at the funeral and the next time that he remembers seeing him was when Charles' was crying softly by his bedside, in the hospital, while he was on the ventilator. Alex is both lost and confused. He does not know how or what to say to his father."

Talk about messed up relationships. Charles' had a great kid and Alex had a great dad and both did not know how to overcome the shadows that enveloped them.

"Sonali, do you think you need to talk to Charles?"

Sonali's expression changed. "Talk to Charles?" The thought seemed to unnerve her. "I don't know. Alex has unburdened himself to me. He needs to talk to his father directly. And well, Charles tends to snub me and has been rude at times. While on the other hand Raghu has stayed in touch over time and is such a sweetheart."

Raghu walked in cutting off further conversation. "There you are, I was wondering where my two favourite girls had wandered off to. Sonali, I can drop you off now, if you are ready."

A knife turned in my side as the two of them bid me farewell and walked off laughing and talking. I was also left wonhdering at Sonali's comment about how Raghu was 'such a sweetheart'.

32

The next day, I was pleasantly surprised to see Charles and Alex actually exchange pleasantries. The plasters were to come off and physiotherapy would commence soon. I had convinced Charles to keep Alex in the hospital as all the time that Sonali was spending with Alex was helping.

Alex had been surprised to hear that his dad's relationship with us went back over two decades to the time we were in medical school together. He enjoyed our banter and taunts. More than that he really enjoyed hearing about our escapades, especially the one in which our pharmacy professor had been treated to itching powder on his table and chair. It had become common for all four of us to collectively and individually spend time with Alex.

Although, Alex was opening up, laughing and joining the conversation every once in a way he could be observed giving his dad questioning looks as though he still didn't know what to make of him.

I spoke to Charles and said, "I think you need to talk to Alex, I mean really talk to him."

His face clouded. "We are able to manage conversations, are actually able to discuss generalities but somehow, both of us are avoiding the personal."

"Try harder. Both of you need to bury the past."

Just then Sonali walked in saying, "Anuja..." Her voice trailed off as she observed me talking to Charles in hushed tones. She turned and left without a word.

I had noticed that Sonali was not comfortable around Charles. She avoided eye contact with him and avoided addressing him directly. On his part, he had been cold initially, but after seeing her interaction with Alex, he had become somewhat tolerant,

Charles sighed, "What's with Sonali? We used to be so close, I still miss her," he said.

Well, well, it seemed like Charles and Raghu were both vying for her attention, poor old me.

"Guess you need to talk to her?"

Leaving Charles with Alex, I headed for the cafeteria two corridors away, where I was to meet Sonali. The place we had chosen was quiet giving us a chance to talk peacefully. Their mind-blowing chicken grilled sandwiches and espresso coffee only made the place more attractive.

I was lost in thought as I reached our rendezvous point. Something of what I was thinking about must have shown on my face. One look, and Sonali wanted to know why I was so melancholic.

"No nothing really, I got off the wrong side of the bed I guess." I couldn't quite tell her that I was actually jealous of all the attention she was getting. I mean I was already upset with myself for thinking uncharitable thoughts about her. She had also been through a lot and definitely deserved happiness.

I just hugged her and got hugged in return.

"Anuja, one look at your face and one can tell that there is something wrong. You haven't grown up in a lot of ways."

"Thanks a lot! That's what my mom keeps telling me. With you, I really feel at home even while being away from home," I said, a wry expression on my face. "Oh hell, thanks for reminding me, I had promised to return my mom's call and never quite got around to it. Give me a second."

"Hi, ma you had called. Yes, I know that was two days ago. I was supposed to call back. I am sorry." I held the cell away from my ear as she continued bombarding me. I rolled my eyes as I looked at Sonali.

After giving my mom enough time to vent herself, I said, "Yes ma, I am sorry. I should have called. It was very irresponsible of me. What is the matter? Is all well?

"Yes, yes, I know the wedding is this weekend. I will be there. Please tell all the auntyjis to lay off. I want to be able to enjoy the wedding and not keep an eye out for shortlisted boys and possible moms-in-law. Don't worry I have arranged the schedule such that I will be there for all the functions.

"Love you too. Take care and let me know if you need me to get anything from here, bye. Take care."

As I disconnected, I realised that Sonali had lost her smile and looked sad. I covered her hand with mine.

"Hey, what's up?"

"You are very lucky to have such supportive parents. Mine have cut me off. I know they still love me, it's more of societal pressure, and my sisters have married into very orthodox families. Dad supported me all through the divorce and in fact kept asking me to come home. I needed to be on my own, and resisted. Now I wish I had gone back."

"I am sure they will accept you with open arms even now.

After all a divorce is not the end of the world." "Not after..." she trailed off.

"After what, Sonali? Stop riddling me."

I was fast losing my patience with all this secrecy. I seemed to land up with only questions where she was concerned.

"Well..."

"Ring, ring..." damn the phone, it had a way of going off at the most inopportune of times.

I answered with a harsh, "Yes."

"Boy am I waiting to be greeted with a friendly hello on the phone once in a while. Is it just me or do you answer it that way every time?" Raghu.

I cursed myself. Here I was waiting for him to call, and I always ended up biting his head off when he did.

"No, no, I am sorry," I said, moving away from Sonali to talk.

"Remember, I had mentioned Mr. Verma to you some time ago? If you could fix up an appointment with him in the next day or so, I would really appreciate it."

"I remember," tucking a stray strand of hair behind my ear, I said, "expect a call in half-an-hour."

"Thanks, will wait for your call." Sigh, not quite the call I was waiting for.

Sonali had ordered for both of us and in fact the order had arrived by the time I made it back to the table.

"Raghu?"

"Uh..."

"Well, Anuja you have been a real rock and very supportive to all of us. In fact, after much deliberation I am going to share with you what I have only shared with my therapist. I want to bury my past good and proper."

"You know I told you that Shubham and I divorced. Well, I very conveniently forgot to tell you what happened between the last time I met Shubham and filed for divorce."

I knew it; there had to be more given the way she had hesitated when narrating how events had played out between her and Shubham.

Sonali continued, "I decided to stick around in Delhi and continue working as I had been. I did not want to go back to my parents knowing the environment there. My sisters had just married. I did not want my marital status to be constantly underlined by my presence at home.

"After about a month of my telling Shubham that we needed to talk if he wanted to get back together, Shubham called back. I had just scrubbed out after a caesarean section. He seemed to be sober, 'Sonali, I am sorry about everything,' he said, 'If you want to talk we will talk. Have dinner with me Saturday evening at Hotel Raj Hans at nine?'

"My heart soared. My first instinct was to refuse. But, to tell you the truth, I really loved Shubham and actually felt sorry for him. He had his weaknesses but well, love is blind I guess. I convinced myself that I had nothing to lose and on an impulse agreed to the meeting. In fact, I was on top of the world. 'Yes, yes,' I said. After I disconnected I felt like I was floating on air. I convinced myself in those five minutes that Shubham and I were getting back together.

"That was a Thursday. It gave me two days to visit the parlour and pick a new dress. I had lots to do before Saturday."

She looked at me, "I'm a sucker for punishment is what you are thinking, right?"

Sonali seemed to be travelling travel back in time, "I pampered myself; did the hair spa, reflexology, massage, facial— the works! In fact I even went shopping for a new dress that would appeal to Shubham. I still loved him a lot. Anyway on the Saturday of the dinner, I fussed over my appearance. Come eight thirty, I was at the Raj Hans, all dressed to kill. I wore a black dress with a sexy slit, my hair piled up with a few stray strands trailing down my beck, I carried a black clutch and wore stilettos. I was oozing confidence. I reached the place and found Ravi and Prem, Shubham's friends waiting for me. They told me that Shubham had been delayed but assured me that he was on the way. They happened to be in the vicinity when he had called and offered to receive me and make me comfortable in the meanwhile. Now I was beginning to regret my choice of dress and the meeting as a whole. Anyway, since I was already there I decided to wait for Shubham," she said, her voice faltering.

"I shrugged off my unease. Shubham probably felt uncomfortable meeting me alone and had called his friends to break the ice. We proceeded to the restaurant. They ordered drinks while we waited. I settled for a diet coke. I was getting restless. I excused myself to go to the cloakroom and tried calling Shubham... His phone was out of range.

"Where was the guy?

"I went back to the table having resolved to leave in the next ten minutes if Shubham did not show up. I made small talk, finished my drink..." her voice trailed off again.

Then she kept silent for a bit as though she was choosing her next words very carefully. She resumed her story, speaking in a small voice, soft and barely audible. When she spoke she choked down a sob and said, "The next thing I remember was waking up in a hotel room with a throbbing headache, alone and half naked. She wrapped both her arms around herself and rocked forward and backward as she relived the scene.

I was too stunned to even react. What? Sonali smiled a watery smile.

"I somehow got my things together. With my shoes in my hand I somehow found my way home. I probably hired a cab. My memory of that morning is a bit hazy. My drink had been spiked, I had been raped."

I drew in a sharp breath.

Sonali continued as if she had not noticed my reaction, "I reached home and remember getting into the shower fully clothed and scrubbing myself till my skin hurt. Tears, water, blood, everything flowed as one. I do not know how long I sat there or anything thereafter. I seemed to just switch myself off. The one person I had trusted with my life had let me down. I shut off my phone, reported sick and the next couple of days are a blur. I slept and I wept for almost a week I guess till my aunt came looking for me. She had called the hospital and had been told that I had reported sick. She took one look at me and knew something was very wrong and actually moved in with me when I refused to leave my apartment. She asked no questions, she fed me, hugged me when I cried, answered the door, took care of visitors and called the hospital to extend my leave. She was just there even though I had nothing to offer her as an explanation. After a couple of days I managed to tell her what had probably happened. She was at her abusive best and wanted me to report the matter to the police. Knowing how rape cases get handled, I refused.

"She decided to scout around on her own. Call it divine providence, but justice was delivered in an unexpected way. Apparently the Honda City that Prem and Ravi were in on the night of the incident had burst a tyre, probably when they were heading home. It had turned turtle since they had been speeding, resulting in a crash that ensured an instantaneous death for Prem. Ravi was in a vegetative brain dead state for a few hours. He died four to eight hours after being hospitalized. A case of accidental death had been registered."

She looked up with a wry expression on her face, "Shubham the bastard, had run into debts and to support his drunkenness had actually pimped me to his friends. Something died inside me that night. I felt no emotions, no anger, no hatred... just nothing. What I did do was call a divorce lawyer and file for a divorce.

"I never communicated in any way with Shubham after that. I heard a couple of years later that he had suffered from end- stage liver failure and had succumbed to his illness. In fact, it was only after hearing that, that I have been able to come out of my trauma of that night and other than my therapist you are the only one in whom I have confided my story.

"Anuja, I changed in that one week. Now there was only Dr. Sonali Dhillon, the workaholic."

We sat in pin-drop silence, my hand on hers. I was struggling to digest the magnitude of the situation and the experiences that Sonali had just revealed to me. Anyone else would have just given up.

Damn the phone. It was my surgeon calling to tell me that the blood for the bypass case had been arranged and I could call the patient to the OT and start.

Sonali had paid the cheque and was gathering her things in preparation to leave. We said our byes and parted ways after exchanging a hug.

33

The patient who was to be operated on was Mr. Verma, the gentleman that Raghu had called about. That truth is stranger than fiction was a saying that I had always mocked but after hearing the stories I had, I had begun to believe otherwise.

Being a cardiac anaesthesiologist, it has always crossed my mind that anyone who reaches the operating table for a coronary bypass surgery must have a trigger factor, which upsets the apple cart so to speak. I mean, no one develops blockages in the blood vessels that supply the heart overnight; the blocks could have been in place for days, yet the attack happens in the present moment.

Mr. Verma was a happily married man. He was a bank official married to a lovely girl who was a teacher and they were blessed with an intelligent three-year-old, Aarti. A perfect life, perfect family. The family had gone for a holiday and returned a day earlier than expected. The night they arrived, thieves entered their house. Mrs. Verma refused to part with the cupboard keys and was stabbed to death in front of her husband and daughter who were tied to chairs. Somehow, the neighbours had sounded an alarm and the thieves were caught. They were in league with the couple's house help. Expecting the family to be away, the robbery had been planned that night. Mr. Verma did not recover from the trauma. In fact, realising that he could not look after his daughter alone in Mumbai, he had sent Aarti to his mother in Rajasthan. Now, five years later, he had met a girl who could not conceive and had agreed to marry him and look after Aarti like a mother. She was a very sweet lady. But now, Aarti refused to leave her grandmother and accept the stepmother. That, for Mr. Verma was now a constant source of concern and the stress had probably triggered an attack and landed him in hospital for surgery.

I met up with Mr. Verma before he was wheeled into the theatre, and told him that he was going to be fine. I was talking to him as I put him under, "Vermaji start counting backwards from ten..."

Ten, nine, eight... Even as he drifted off his last thought was, "Hope Aarti comes home."

The surgery went off well. While in the theatre I learnt that one of our recovery room nurses had resigned overnight. The reason was Dr. Abhinav. The theatre was abuzz with the news that Dr. Abhinav had married someone from our recovery room staff.

Wonders never cease. Dr. Abhinav was easily touching his retirement age. He was 5ft 11 inches tall, had a waistline of at least 48 inches, was married to a lovely dentist colleague, and had three teenage daughters all enrolled in various professional courses. The staff member in question was a nubile eighteen-year-old. What had she been thinking? Love was blind in the truest sense of the word.

The incongruity of the situation was just too much to digest and it seemed a little difficult to accept the news. Ooh! But that was only till fresh news started streaming in that Dr. Abhinav had actually thrown a just-wedded party and invited only a select few colleagues. One of our senior surgeons couldn't help but comment, "He could have had her, I mean, that I can understand. But did he have to marry her?"

Hospitals are never short of excitement and the grapevine is just waiting for juicy gossip. Today was my day for an information overload. My head was spinning; I needed to hit the gym to release my emotions. Sonali's story had really disturbed me.

I felt such a heel for thinking the way I had about Sonali. She deserved happiness. In that moment, I wished that if Raghu was her happiness it should happen.

But that evening, I couldn't help but stand in front of my full length mirror and ask my not-too-bad reflection why people (read the guys) forgot that I also existed.

34

Alex had been discharged. He'd had a grand party arranged for him by the recovery staff. He had won them all over, and had become quite the heartthrob of the younger lot. They were all extremely happy at his recovery and wished him well.

Charles had arranged a quiet dinner for all of us at his place. Alex loved the house. His dad had taken extreme pains to do up Alex's room the way he loved it. It was the right shade of blue, had a king-size bed, all of his football memorabilia, and his favourite life-size photograph with his mom and dad along with his first football trophy. Alex gave his dad a spontaneous hug and whispered a soft "Thanks" into his ear as he drew away. Charles was ecstatic.

The evening was a ball. Everyone was relaxed and happy, and all our guards were down. Charles and Sonali seemed to have made their peace. Our take-away dinner had been devoured and we were all lounging in the living room. A nice track by Fausto Pappetti was playing in the background.

Charles suddenly looked at Alex and said, "Son, there is something I need to share with you. I am unable to say it when we are alone. I would like to make the confession in front of my friends."

Alex nodded, almost as if he had expected nothing else.

"The night that your mother, Victoria, died I had been working on an extremely high-risk case and had finished only around 9:30 pm. Victoria had been calling every minute from quarter past nine and had left extremely abusive messages on my voice mail. I was very tired mentally and physically, and her messages only served to irritate me. I guess I should have ignored them and waited till I got home. Instead I called her. I was pissed.

"When she answered, her speech was slurred, I realised she was drunk. She started abusing me and threatened to first kill me and then herself. I told her that I was fed up too and she should do just that and disconnected.

"After putting the phone down and cooling off a bit, I realised that she had sounded really wild. I tried calling back. My calls were not answered. My first instinct was to stay away for the night, but I was worried, I had to get home as fast as I could. Cursing myself for the way I had spoken to her I ran out to my car. Thanks to a pile up on the expressway, the half-an-hour drive took two hours."

"It was possible that Victoria was waiting for me. The moment I entered she walked out to the first floor landing with a wild look in her eyes; I realised she was really drunk. She started abusing me, and rushed towards me. I yelled for her to be careful. Even as I uttered the words I saw her trip on her nightgown. She rolled all the way down the stairs."

"I was stunned! I see blood every day, handle blood every day. But to see Victoria splayed like that, her blood all over... it was horrible." Charles was visibly moved, his voice broke, and his eyes were haunted, as he seemed to relive the moment.

He shook himself after a moment's silence, saying "And that was when you walked in".

"You were right, I probably did kill her. Maybe if I had kept my cool that day. Just come home earlier or even stayed away, I do not know. But believe me I really loved your mother…" there was a sob in his voice as it trailed off.

There was pin drop silence. Alex picked up his walker, closed the distance and hugged his father. Two souls, a common loss, both convinced that they could have in some way prevented the tragedy.

As if by mutual, unvoiced consent the three of us—Raghu, Sonali, and I, quietly let ourselves out, leaving the emotionally charged father and son to finally grieve together and lay their ghosts to rest.

We all had tears in our eyes. We hugged each other and parted ways in the parking lot.

35

Sonali called me just as I was entering the hospital next morning. "Guess what, Alex called. Charles and he talked into the wee hours of the morning. Father and son have started the healing process.

"In fact, Alex is back to posting messages on Facebook and is extremely happy."

Great, things seemed to be working out. Now it was time to get down to business. Promising to meet Sonali after work, I settled into my operative schedule.

I finished early and, as promised, called Sonali. Raghu answered. I was green with jealousy. What was Raghu doing answering Sonali's phone? "Hi, Raghu here. Sonali is driving. I'll ask her to call you." I was left staring at the phone, thoroughly pissed.

Sonali called after an hour. "Busy bee, nice to know that you have finished early today. I'll pick you up. Wait at the hospital. Be there in five."

No hi, no by the way, no do you have other plans, well... I didn't have any so I waited.

Everyone around seemed to have a life, except me. Time to pick yourself up-take that holiday to Egypt or that Nile cruise

I had read about… or get a personal trainer… and a face lift maybe… get an entire image change. Sonali's arrival interrupted my black thoughts.

Sonali was extremely excited and animated. She had met Charles and Alex for lunch. Then gone to Forum to check it out where she had bumped into Raghu and given him a lift back. Ah, so that explained Raghu, I was still upset for no apparent reason. "Let's go to Coffee Café Day, find a quiet table. I have so much to tell you!"

She seemed ecstatic. "It has been a great day. Anuja, Charles has been so rude and abrupt with me that I was beginning to think that I should stay away from him. But well, we have managed to sort things out. And Raghu," a pause, a dreamy look later, "He is the best. I don't know what I would do without him."

Oh, oh, where was this going?

Over coffee, Sonali started telling me how much happier Alex was looking, he seemed to have transformed overnight. And oh, so casually, she said, "Before I forget, I am getting engaged." Just then her mobile rang.

A hurried hi and yeah on the phone later, she said, "Anuja, I have to run, it's an emergency, Raghu is waiting outside." She sailed out; all this with a grin that ran ear to ear and a glow that couldn't contain itself.

Getting engaged, just like that; Raghu waiting outside? I was left with my mouth hanging wide open. I was mad, I hate not knowing what is going on. Mumbling to myself about friends who take you for granted and cursing my luck, I made my way home after settling the tab.

Every meeting with Sonali left me feeling like I had been on a roller-coaster ride. Engaged! I was dying to call and find out to whom. But damn it, I could not even call and ask, my ego got in the way, as usual. Hell!

I could not concentrate on anything after that. I fretted and fretted, wondering to whom Sonali was getting engaged. But of course I did not call to find out. Everyone behaved as though it was quite obvious who Sonali's fiancé was and that I must know it.

Raghu called me, "Anuja, we are all dining together tonight to celebrate the engagement. No excuses, we are meeting at nine."

My worst fears were being realised.

Raghu. I died a thousand deaths. After all these years there's only been one guy that I have ever been interested in and have always been interested in, and now he was getting engaged, AGAIN… and this time to one of my best friends.

I had a wild thought of excusing myself from the occasion under the pretext of work. I chided myself. Are you planning to cut them out of your life again? If not, the earlier you deal with the situation the better. We were adults after all. You have to be happy for friends. I smiled wryly as I considered my options. What the hell, it's always more fun getting drunk in company, at least you will get dropped home safely!

"Oh wow, that's great. I'll definitely be there, the champagne is on me."

Somehow the Trident seemed to have become our celebration ground.

I took time off and decided to get the make-over I had been planning. I tried everything they had to offer-manicure, pedicure, haircut, streaks and a facial-and hoped that this would improve my mood. The only problem was that I did not feel any different; it still hurt on the inside. Nonetheless, I made it a point to dress to kill.

For once, I was the last to put in an appearance. I paused to observe the group; the table was overflowing with happiness. Charles, Raghu and Alex were all looking dapper. They had turned up in their Sunday best, dressed to kill. Sonali, as usual, looked elegantly dressed in a backless, black gown. Even sans make-up, she looked like a goddess. Every male in that room was doing a double take when she walked by.

All four were laughing their head off. The instinct to turn and run away was very strong. I had to steel my every nerve to stay. Alex was the first to spot me and he gave a wolf whistle. The kid made my day, I felt better already. Charles pulled out a chair for me and asked the maître d' to bring the champagne bottle while giving Sonali a look. I gave Charles a funny look in turn. I mean even though he was still soft on Sonali he seemed happy with the idea of Raghu beating him to it. He was probably putting on a brave front like me. I gave him a sympathetic look that said, "I know how you feel," which seemed to puzzle him.

The champagne arrived. Alex pulled out a jewellers' box from his coat pocket. What was going on? Alex and Sonali? I was drunk without drinking. Raghu gave Sonali an affectionate look and laid his hand on hers. Raghu and Sonali?

My head was spinning. Exactly what was going on? Imagine my surprise when Charles knelt down in front of Sonali and Alex handed him the ring.

Total disbelief. I did not know whether to laugh or cry. But my cheeks were definitely wet and tears were rolling down along with the mascara.

Charles and Sonali got a standing ovation and a lot of best wishes from the other patrons. Charles, being what he is, stood up and announced that the liquor bill for the entire restaurant was on him that evening. A cheer went up.

There was a lot of laughing and crying. The Trident staff brought out an impromptu engagement cake, the live band took its cue and only old romantic songs were played. It was a dream evening. I was real happy for Charles, Sonali, and Alex. These guys had been through a lot and needed some real happiness. It emerged that Charles had booked the three of them on an African Safari. All else could wait.

And me? Yippee! Raghu was still a free man. The night was a blur. I don't even remember being dropped home!

36

The next day, I got up on a high. The events of the earlier evening still felt surreal. Yet they had restored my faith in all things good.

I literally sang and danced through my morning routine. Everyone in hospital stopped and complimented me on my new look. I even got Dr. Rakesh, all of sixty and a confirmed bachelor to say, "Wow, I would marry you today if you would have me". Nothing like compliments to keep you on cloud nine.

The next couple of days were an anticlimax given the whirl of activity that had preceded them. Raghu seemed to have disappeared off the face of the earth after the engagement party. I started wondering if I had misread the entire situation. Maybe Raghu had been sweet on Sonali and the engagement had actually upset him? Charles, Sonali, and Alex had left for their exotic African holiday. Sigh, I seemed to be back to square one- my boring, routine life. Get up in the morning, go to work, get back home, sit in front of the idiot box, and go to bed.

I couldn't get Raghu out of my head. I picked up my phone on a couple of occasions to dial Raghu, but each time failed to hit the dial button.

I was to leave on the weekend for Pune. My mom seemed to be volunteering our home as a venue for all upcoming wedding celebrations as well as for dekho sessions with prospective brides and grooms. Probably compensating for the opportunity I made her miss. Mom, I really love you.

I was really looking forward to going home. I had initially planned to take the car, but for some reason decided to give the Indian Railways a chance to provide me a carriage. It was a quiet day at work and I had already handed over for the weekend. In fact I had decided to make it a long weekend and reach in time for the mehendi and sangeet (ceremonies prior to the wedding). Oh, my cousin was getting married. A chartered accountant, she was marrying her colleague from Parulekar and Sons, a Chartered Accountant firm. Both families were from Pune.

Feeling extremely charitable, I repacked my bag to include some really pretty saris and my ghagra. Mom needed a break. The only thing that nagged me was that Raghu had made no effort to contact me since the night of the engagement. Well, maybe I should call. I picked up the phone, even dialed his number but cut it before it rang. I decided to wait a while.

The Deccan Queen was on time, both in its departure from Mumbai and its arrival in Pune. I used the journey to catch up on my music and picked up at least five kilos of chikki (a caramelised sweet) from Lonavala. I took an auto from the station. I wanted to give Mom a surprise.

Loaded with luggage I reached home to find the whole house decorated. A pandal with an entrance that resembled the entrance of the Taj adorned our entrance and was encroaching the road. Wow, talk about going overboard. I was quite looking forward to the rest of the wedding.

Although… an SMS that had been doing the rounds lately suddenly came back to me:

We all know the Taj Mahal to be a symbol of Eternal Love... But the lesser known facts are:

Mumtaz was SHAHJAHAN'S 4th wife, OUT OF HIS SEVEN WIVES.

Shahjahan killed Mumtaz's husband to marry her. Mumtaz died during her 14th delivery.

Shahjahan then married Mumtaz's sister. Where the hell is the love here, please explain! I smiled to myself; "Sour grapes, Anuja?"

As I was paying off the auto guy, out of the corner of my eye I spotted someone in blue jeans and a white t-shirt supervising some last minute decoration changes. Imagine my surprise when I realised it was Raghu! I was stunned. What in heaven's name was he doing here?

Without a Hi, or a How are you, he just plucked the bags from my hands and started walking towards the house. I practically ran after him, "Hey, wait up. What are you doing here? When did you come?"

Raghu just smiled as we entered the house. I was immediately surrounded by family, all hugging me and talking at the same time. My mom, who was giving instructions to the help, stopped mid-sentence and came running to embrace me. "I am so glad you came early. Freshen up and come give me a hand. There is so much to be done. I will get you a cup of tea in the meanwhile."

I peeped in on dad in his den, sitting with all the "uncles". They were laughing loudly. Both literally and metaphorically speaking, their spirits were high. Dad raised his eyebrows when he saw me at the door and he came across and gave me a quick hug before I proceeded to my room.

I changed out of my jeans into a salwar and took pains with my appearance. God damn it, what was Raghu doing here?

I returned to where all the action was and soon got busy stringing flowers and supervising dinner preparations. I did not see Raghu around. Was I going mad? Had I just imagined his presence? I turned around, a huge plate of ladoos (an Indian sweet) in my hand, and there he was. He promptly took the plate out of my hand and said, "Hi, let me help you."

"What are you doing here?"

Raghu was enjoying both my discomfort and surprise, "Attending a wedding, remember."

Like that eh! "Yes, but who invited you." "Auntyji, your mother."

Now, I was really confused."When did she meet you? When did she invite you? How come no one mentioned it to me?"

Just then my mom came by. "Raghu beta, please take the ladoos outside, everyone is waiting."

Very obediently Raghu trotted off, turning momentarily to wink at me.

Now I was mad.

"Mamma..." all I got was a smile as she hurried off.

It was about an hour later that my mom came to me and said, "Anuja, the tailor was supposed to have given your dress today. Now that you are here, you can go yourself, try it on and get any alterations done if you want to. Be out in five minutes, I will make sure that a car is waiting for you."

Moms will be moms. I changed my footwear and in five minutes I obediently made my way to the door. Imagine my surprise when I found Raghu waiting for me. He gave me his arm and said, "Ma'am your carriage awaits." He saw my hand go to my hair and my face register an expression that said, "Oh my God I hope I look okay" and just smiled a knowing smile.

He drove me to the tailors and sat through the trials very patiently. In fact he almost seemed to be enjoying himself. He actually participated by giving us his suggestions! The tailor visit over, I sat in the passenger seat lost in thought.

The journey so far had been completed in silence. I was sulking and Raghu was enjoying the situation. Every once in a while I caught him looking at me and smiling. Damn him.

I suddenly realised we were travelling towards Deccan, in the opposite direction from home. "Raghu, I guess you have lost your way." Raghu just smiled and continued to drive in the opposite direction.

We landed up at the Boat Club. "Raghu we need to be getting back."

"Anuja just relax. We are having dinner here."

"Raghu, there is a wedding happening at home." I was really agitated now.

"Anuja, chill, we will be back before the action starts."

I stood undecided for a moment. Then just shrugged and gave in. I decided to take Raghu's advice to chill and enjoy the situation.

Raghu had booked a table for two. Our Chinese meal and drinks were already ordered. He'd ordered all my favourites.

"Hope the favourites haven't changed?" he said as the steward reconfirmed our order. A nod confirmed his choice. Raghu never ceased to amaze me, considering that the last Chinese meal we had shared as a couple had been in college.

He then proceeded to pluck the red rose gracing the centre of the table and hand it to me, "For my favourite girl."

The wine arrived and he made a toast, "Here's to friends and friendship."

"Anuja, tell me honestly, you thought I was the one that Sonali was getting engaged to, right?"

I went red in the face. I couldn't look him straight in the eye.

Damn Raghu, he always put me in a spot.

Raghu seemed to sober up. He sighed and said "I guess it's time I answered all your questions."

Now he had me confused, "Questions? Answered?"

"I know you have a lot of questions that you are dying to ask and either don't know how to ask or whom to ask."

"Well, let's start with… after a significant pause, Manju?" I sat upright, "How do you …"

"Remember, Charles and Sonali were working in the same institute at Delhi. Charles always had a crush on her…" (Yeah sure! So did the entire medical college including you)

"Charles had never been able to disclose his feelings to Sonali. He was worried that he might also lose her as a friend in the bargain.

"To cut a long story short, while in Delhi during the time that Sonali and Shubham had a fall out, Charles was the shoulder she cried on. She was extremely fragile emotionally. Charles actually started wooing her. One evening while at a party, they got drunk and the evening ended in Charles' room.

"When Sonali realised what had happened, she was aghast. She took a long medical leave, feigning an attack of typhoid. And within a fortnight she sent in her resignation.

"Charles was devastated. He tried everything he could to find her but failed miserably. Meanwhile, the American medical scholarship he had been waiting for materialised. He was given a joining time of three weeks. With things stacked against him as they were, Charles accepted the offer. He kept hoping against hope that Sonali would show up, she didn't.

"In a couple of weeks, Sonali realised that the one night stand had resulted in a conception. She was shaken. Considering her conservative background, the fact that she had two unmarried sisters at home and the social implications and possible stigma, she tried to trace Charles. When she learnt that he had left for God only knows how long and without a forwarding address, she decided to get an abortion." "That is how she reached your hospital," he said shrugging, "... and well, you know the rest."

"How do you know all this?"

"I remembered your comment about how Sonali was uncomfortable around Charles. I mentioned it to Sonali jokingly and she got all serious on me and refused to talk to me at all till I promised not to probe.

"Then yesterday, when I was helping Charles to finalize his travel plans, he confided in me. He told me that Sonali and he had bared their hearts to each other and were ready to make a clean start. Sonali in fact had also requested Charles to tell us the entire story if he felt comfortable, since in some ways we were all in this together.

"Sonali apparently had tried to tell you her complete story but somehow circumstances had deigned otherwise."

The whole jigsaw suddenly fell in place.

"Charles has had a rough time. He's extremely happy for being given this second chance and having Alex back to bless his decision was the icing on the cake.

"And now ma'am, enough talk, lets enjoy our dinner and take a moonlit stroll."

Talk about life being a b***h. The quirkiness of it all was astounding—Sonali an IVF specialist, gets married and has issues with getting pregnant because of Shubham's problem, yet a one night stand just a few months earlier with Charles had resulted in a pregnancy which had needed an abortion!

I put Charles and Sonali aside as I silently sent up a prayer for the three of them and settled down to enjoy the dinner and the company.

I could not help but ask, "Where have you been since their engagement?"

"Preparing for the wedding, of course." His eyes twinkled. "Now for the other thing that has been bothering you, trying to figure out what I am doing here in Pune. Incidentally, your cousin is marrying Ketan who is a good friend and a chartered accountant; in fact he has been helping me with my financial issues since I decided to move back to India. I could hardly refuse, could I?" he said with a twinkle in his eye.

That explained it. "But what about mom?"

"I just introduced myself to her, told her I was a good friend of yours. She welcomed me with a big hug." Boy, was my mother gullible. Anyone goes to her and tells her they are my good friend and she welcomes them into the family fold, with open arms! Crazy. I needed to talk to her.

"Oh, and before I forget. I have finalised my shift to Mumbai. I officially join Forum Hospital in a month."

"They are waiting for you to make up your mind," he said with a chuckle.

The dinner was great; in fact it was perfect. Both of us did not feel the need for unnecessary chatter. We just relaxed in each other's company; enjoying each other and the music. Every time I looked up I saw Raghu looking at me with a mysterious smile on his lips. On finishing dinner, he very chivalrously helped me out of my chair. I was on top of the world. We walked along the lake. The night was perfect, there was a full moon to light our path, the skies were clear, studded with glistening diamonds. The moonlight reflected off the quiet waters of the lake. It was as if only the two of us existed.

He took my hand as we walked, " Anuja, you do realize that you mean a lot to me. I have put my demons to rest and am finally ready to move on."

I sighed as Raghu put his arm around me, and snuggled in. It seemed the right thing to do. Raghu took my hand in his and kissed it.

Kissing one finger at a time he said, "Incidentally, I also spoke to your parents and they are happy to accept me as their son-in-law. In fact your mother is eagerly looking forward to planning and executing her daughter's wedding, finally."

Oh, the shivers that ran down my spine. "But..."

Raghu put a finger across my lips as he caressed them gently, "Shh...enough of your buts. Anuja, I love you. Marry me."